WORLDS
WITHIN

By
ROG PHILLIPS

ARMCHAIR FICTION
PO Box 4369, Medford, Oregon 97504

*For more information about Armchair Books and products, visit our
website at…*

www.armchairfiction.com

Or email us at…

armchairfiction@yahoo.com

DOORWAYS TO OTHER WORLDS...

Carter was an engineer engaged in top secret research at Lockheed. He was shaving one morning when a knock came at his apartment door and a drop-dead beautiful girl pushed it open before he could reach it himself. That was to be the first of many doors she would open for him. In rapid succession, out-of-this-world adventures took him through the dangers and breathtaking wonders of realms undreamed of by science—yet described with amazing accuracy by works that were supposed to be pure fiction!

Worlds within worlds, through door after door, his love for this girl drew him on. But the last door was the most dangerous of all. To close that door Carter had to close his heart against his love in a solemn pact with a woman of another realm who held, for one awful moment, the power to doom all mankind—and she bargained it for Carter's soul!

FOR A SECOND COMPLETE NOVEL, TURN TO PAGE 149

CAST OF CHARACTERS

LIN CARTER

Being a top engineer from his era, he was called upon to help save the world. But which world would he choose to save?

EDONA MORELL

She was a gutsy young woman who proved to be as bold in action as she was naïve in love.

ARTAXL

Battle scarred and fearsome to look upon, yet his evil appearance might be misleading.

RAX ANTL

A noble leader of Incan descent, he was prepared to give his life in order to save more that just his own people.

MARA

She was a married woman, but this conniving troublemaker didn't care. If she wanted you—she got you.

MONTAKOTL

The last of the Incan Emperors, he held the key to closing a door to evil forever—but he was a coward.

ARTHUR GATES

He was a reporter following a lead—the story of a lifetime! But would he live long enough to tell it?

CHAPTER ONE

THE KNOCK at the door was sharp, demanding. Lin Carter frowned his annoyance, gave his face a last, critical inspection before shutting off his electric razor. Today would see the completion of the XB56 stratofighter he had played a major part in designing at Lockheed. Any interruptions that would delay his getting to work were the last thing he wanted.

The knocking stopped. Whoever was out in the hall rattled the knob impatiently, back and forth. The inevitable happened. The door opened slightly. There was a split second of silence as the person outside digested the fact that it had not been locked.

Lin had almost reached the door when it was flung open. There was a blur of motion, the slam of the door as it was violently closed, a slim hand twisting the night latch.

The slim hand connected to a slender wrist and white arm that disappeared into the loose short sleeve of a dress. A well-formed nose was flaring perceptibly as it sucked in lungsfull of air. Blue eyes filled with excitement were framed by dark lashes. Rich blonde hair held generous, glistening waves.

All these isolated, startled impressions that struck into Lin's mind settled into one picture, of a girl about twenty-one, half a head shorter than his five eleven. A girl he had never seen before—and who was obviously afraid of something. The most beautiful girl he had ever seen—and she was wearing a strange belt about her slim waist, and what seemed to be a parachute pack on her shoulders!

His eyes shifted questioningly from the parachute pack to the belt. Her left hand, concealed behind her, came into view and lifted toward him urgently. It held a belt identical with the one she wore. She held it out to him. Her lips opened as if she were about to speak. Her eyes were round, pleading.

The knob started to rattle again. There was a strained creak as someone tried to push the door open, a dull thud as the panel was hit by a solid shoulder.

Lin had reached out to take the belt in the girl's hand. She stepped away from him, shaking her head, her eyes darting around the room.

There was another heavy blow against the door. She crossed to the davenport and lifted a pillow, hiding the belt under it.

A third blow splintered the panel, knocking it loose in its frame. Heavy fingers came into view, straining, ripping at the torn plywood. It came loose. Two men pushed through into the room.

Lin's eyes switched to the girl, then became round. Very round. What he was seeing was impossible.

As his eyes focused on her she was sinking into the floor. The thick carpet chopped off her legs at the knees. She was apparently falling right through solid matter as if it weren't there at all! Her legs vanished. Her body was disappearing. For an instant she was just a bust melting into the floor, a look of concentration on its face. Her blonde hair blended with the rug design at the last instant. She was gone.

Lin's attention went back to the two men. Each had run toward the girl. Now they jumped into the air like two divers springing off a board. Each fumbled at the belt he wore. Then each reached over his shoulder to a round ring on his left shoulder and pulled.

Their legs went into the floor as small white parachutes slid out of packs and billowed open. The two men were fading into nothingness before they had gone out of sight into the floor.

Lin found himself waiting for a ripple in the surface of the rug. He took a deep breath and wondered if he had gone insane. Perhaps this was what insanity was like—quite a bit different than he had always thought it might be.

But no, there was the belt the girl had hidden under the davenport pillow. He crossed the room and took it from its hiding place. It was real.

It was of dark canvas, doubled over, with something thick and flat inside. One of its ends was a buckle-like plate with three holes in its end. The other end of the belt terminated in three prongs of a dark metal. They were evidently supposed to slip into the three holes, like a plug into a wall outlet.

The part of the belt that would be in front, if it were put on, was about two inches wide and almost a half-inch thick. In the back it widened to six inches, with a round-cornered box sewn in. The box might be a power pack of some sort.

Lin's eyes studied the small pegs in the buckle. The girl and the two men had pushed on one of those pins before sinking through the floor.

Should he put on the belt and follow them? What would happen? Those parachutes billowing open suggested great heights—and Lin's room was on the second floor of a brick apartment house, with one floor below, then solid ground from there to the center of the Earth, so far as he knew!

He swung the belt around his waist and caught the other end. The belt nestled snugly against his back. He held the three-pronged end against its matching holes in the buckle, hesitating.

A sound startled him. He looked up. The girl was stepping into the room through the broken panel of the door, a satisfied smile on her lips.

"I outsmarted them," she said. Her voice was smooth. "We'll have to hurry though. They'll be back as soon as they realize I didn't go on down."

Lin noticed that she, too, wore a parachute on her back.

"Where'd you go?" he asked.

"I just slipped through to the room below," she said. "They thought I would keep right on going."

Her eyes took in the belt. She went up to Lin and slipped the prongs into place. There was a slight click as a locking mechanism inside took hold of them.

"Come with me," she said, stepping back. "We can't be here when they come back." Her eyes looked questioningly at him. "You are Lin Carter, aren't you?"

"Yes," Lin said. "And who are you? Ana what is all this?"

"I'm Edona Morell," she said. "You're the Lin Carter that studied under my father, Dr. Morell, at Northwestern in Chicago, aren't you?"

Lin nodded, his face showing startled remembrance. It was his work under Morell that had won him his research job with Lockheed.

"He needs you," Edona said. "Please come with me. There's no time to explain anything. Will you?" Her full, pointed breasts rose and fell rapidly from her tense breathing as he hesitated.

"Sure," Lin said in sudden decision. "My car's parked out in front. We can use that. Where are we going?"

They were out in the hall now, walking close together.

"We've got to find an airport and get a plane," Edona said, tripping down the stairs with Lin beside her. Seconds later they were in the front seat of his car and pulling away from the curb. Her nearness on the seat beside him disturbed Lin. He shoved Lockheed and the XB56 out of his mind.

"There's a private airport just a couple of miles from here in Gardena," Lin said, slipping expertly into the morning traffic of Los Angeles's Western Avenue and heading south.

"Good!" Edona exclaimed with relief. "We'll need a three-seater and pilot—and you'll need a parachute."

Lin reached under the dashboard and drew out a two-way telephone. Shortly he was connected to the airport. He was lucky. There would be a three-seater and pilot ready in five minutes. The plane was already on the field and could be warmed up in that time.

"Now," Lin said firmly as he replaced the car telephone. "What's this all about? Why does your father need me?"

Edona twisted in the seat and looked back.

"Is that a car following us?" she asked anxiously.

Lin studied the car. It was weaving in and out of traffic, creeping closer rapidly.

"Could be," he said grimly. He stepped on the gas and started to dodge around cars as he picked up speed.

"What's this all about?" he repeated his question. Then, "Never mind. Here's the airport."

The car tipped precariously as he turned off Western Avenue onto the side road leading to the field. The pursuing car was less than a city block behind them now.

"We'll drive right out onto the field," Lin said.

His eyes had found the plane with its pilot standing under a wing. The doors swung open under the impetus of stopping. They jumped out and ran to the plane.

"Hurry!" Edona called anxiously to the pilot.

The three of them climbed quickly into the cabin. The pilot started the plane at once. It was lifting its tail in preparation for leaving the ground as the car that followed them skidded to a stop and the two men got out to stand staring after them. The plane lifted and circled.

"Where to?" the pilot asked.

"Oh," Edona said. She looked out the plastic dome of the cabin. "Go up to fourteen thousand feet." She sat erect, her eyes looking at the widening landscape below them. Once her eyes flicked to Lin. "Better put on the chute," she suggested tensely.

The drone of the two motors was a deep, steady roar as the blades bit into the air in a steep climb. The plane was headed north, and was over greater Los Angeles now. It leveled off, the motors softening their sound.

"We're at fourteen thousand now," the pilot said.

"Stay there and turn south," Edona ordered.

She relaxed and inspected Lin's parachute. It was on properly.

"When I jump, follow me," she whispered in Lin's ear. "Press that red pin. It will throw you free of the plane. Then pull the ring on your chute. Try to land where I do."

There was a field of squat oil storage tanks below when Edona's finger pressed the red pin on her belt. Her face held entreaty as she sank through the upholstered seat out of sight.

Lin, feeling a sick sensation in the pit of his stomach, wondered what the pilot would say when he looked back and saw they were gone.

He pressed the red pin. There was a strange blur in his eyes. Terror gripped him as his right hand reached for the ripcord ring and yanked.

Suddenly the plane was above him, queerly changing position as the Earth swung upward in a giant arc. Strong hands grabbed his shoulders and held him.

He was swaying dizzily. The white disc of the chute was above him. Below the Earth had suddenly and unbelievably jumped up so that it was a bare thousand feet below. Where the ocean should be was a mountain whose snowcapped peak went upward.

The dots of oil tanks, the lines of highways, and the plane they had just forsaken, were gone. It was as abrupt as a change of scene in a movie.

To the east a huge red sun hung suspended in the sky. Below were the tops of tall trees rushing up.

Edona was near, hanging in the harness of her own chute. Her voice came across the intervening distance.

"Are you all right, Lin?" she called. "Try to keep near me?"

"I'm O.K.," Lin called. "Where are we?"

"It'll all be explained," Edona answered. "We want to land in that clearing down there so as to miss the treetops."

"All right," Lin called reassuringly. "I know how." He pulled at the shroud-lines and felt the sickening sideslip as he veered to a spot over the clearing—just in time to avoid the trees.

He let his feet take the first force of landing. The smooth expanse of the chute drifted down by him into the tall grass.

"This is all taking place a couple of miles above Los Angeles," he thought. "But if that's so, why did those men have to use parachutes in jumping from my room?"

Edona hadn't cleared the trees enough. Lin got up and went to her rescue where she was dangling a few feet off the ground, an expression of indignation on her face. Before he reached her, her chute slipped free. She landed gracefully.

"Do you know how to fold up a chute?" she asked.

Lin shook his head. Edona busied herself folding both chutes and replacing them in their packs.

"We might have to use them any minute," she said breathlessly. "And we have quite a ways to go yet before we're safe."

Her eyes searched the sky fearfully. She peered through the trees like a wild creature, wary of stalking danger.

"Will you tell me what this is all about now?" Lin asked tiredly.

"Be quiet," Edona said, laying a hand on his arm pleadingly. "There's still danger. Be patient."

CHAPTER TWO

SHE TURNED away abruptly and went toward the edge of the forest that surrounded the clearing. Lin followed her, his eyes on the back of her head, held erect, and her firm shoulders. There seemed to be a courage there, embodied in those shoulders and neck.

Lin felt an impulse to take her in his arms and assure her that whatever was the matter she could be sure of his help. He resisted it, following her closely as she parted some bushes and set foot on a faint path leading toward the mountains.

The bushes were familiar, though Lin had never become familiar enough with any type of wild shrubbery to be able to know whether they were types growing back on the Earth he knew. The trees were something else. Lin felt quite sure they had no counterparts on Earth. Their leaves were almost grass-like; long and extremely narrow, soft and very green. They made the branches of the trees seem bearded rather than leafed.

Edona walked swiftly, her head continually exploring with nervous tenseness. Once there was a loud crashing not far away. Edona dropped quickly to the ground. Lin dropped beside her. She kept her eyes averted, but he saw that she felt his nearness. He became bold and reached out, closing his hand over hers.

The crashing noises had died down in the distance long ago. It was evident that Edona hated to end the intimacy of Lin holding her hand.

Finally it became obvious to her that it was obvious to him. She turned slowly red. Her eyes met Lin's with a timid courage. Then she withdrew her hand and stood up.

"It was only an animal," Lin said matter-of-factly to set her at ease.

"Probably a Quotl," Edona said, her voice matching his. "They're something like a moose. Let's go. We have to reach a village at the base of the mountain. It's another four or five miles yet."

"Your father is there?" Lin asked.

"Yes," Edona said. Her lip trembled.

"Is he ill?" Lin asked.

"He may not live," Edona said. "That's why he sent for you."

"Oh," Lin said lamely. He followed Edona, trying to think of something to say.

The sun climbed higher in the sky. Now and then Lin looked at it thoughtfully. Though the sky was cloudless it was possible to look directly at the sun without being blinded.

Was it the same sun that belonged to the Earth he had left? He was convinced this wasn't the Earth. It couldn't be. If it were the same sun, though, this must be a planet much nearer it than the Earth.

Had the belt around his waist transported him by some unknown science across space to Venus? That didn't quite answer why the sun was only red hot instead of the white inferno the sun of the Earth was.

Lin tried to recall something about Dr. Morell that might be a clue. What had Dr. Morell been interested in? So far as Lin could remember, Dr. Morell had merely been a good teacher of advanced physics, sticking to the class work, not revealing any of his private research in his lectures, though there had been rumors of his doing research for the A. E. C.

Lin finally gave up. There was nothing, absolutely nothing, to indicate where they were—except that they were in a strange world, which must be a couple of miles straight up or down from Los Angeles and the rest of southern California, since they had dropped from a plane without any evidence of having traveled any distance.

The path had a constant upward slope now. Ahead through the trees Lin thought he saw the opening of a ravine into the cliffs that formed the base of the mountain. Also, the path was wider and harder packed from use. Other paths branched into it and away from it.

There was the sound of running water not far away. They came to a place where the path bordered a steep embankment that dropped to a turbulent stream.

They were in the ravine, following the base of the cliff. It pressed in until they were walking along the shore of the river. Now and then the path they walked on became wet from spray and waves.

For a hundred yards their path was nothing but precarious leaps from one jagged boulder to another. Overhead the cliffs that bordered the stream seemed to come together. The air was cold like that from a cave. Then the ravine widened. Far ahead the white cascades of a waterfall could be seen. But nearer was something that attracted Lin's eyes. It was a group of buildings that nestled at the base of the cliff.

They were still at least a quarter of a mile away when Lin first saw them. They looked more like a picture than reality, and were like pictures he had seen of Aztec villages.

Lin and Edona were now walking on soft earth matted with dense growths of wild plants. Nearby was a large patch of buttercups. The sight of them made Lin feel more secure. If there were buttercups it might be the Earth after all, in spite of evidence that denied it.

There was movement ahead. The buildings were no more than two hundred yards away. Half-naked men were running toward them. They wore short apron-like clothes that hung from their waist. Their skins were tanned deeply, or perhaps naturally dark like an Indian's.

Perhaps they were Indians! The possibility came to Lin as a shock. At first he couldn't understand why it should be a shock, then it came to him.

Deep in his subconscious the thought had occurred to him that he might be dead. Subconsciously he had denied the possibility—shied away from it. Yet it was there.

An abrupt, unreal series of actions, beginning as he finished shaving, involving things absolutely impossible according to known science; a crazy trip in a plane that took them high above Los Angeles; a drop into a strange country with even stranger trees, all a couple of miles above the real Earth; and now Indians with the association, happy hunting grounds, and death.

It was fantastic to think he might be dead, yet it could be possible to die so quickly that death wasn't consciously experienced: then if there were life after death—what form would it take? Lin felt a sharp nausea at the realization that he couldn't rule out the possibility of his being dead.

But none of this was revealed on his face as several Indians came to meet them, broad smiles of welcome on their faces. They looked at Lin curiously, giving him a reserved respect with their manner.

Edona spoke to them in a strange language and they answered in the same tongue. The language was clipped, seeming to consist of one-syllable words.

They went on toward the village as they talked. Edona turned to Lin with a smile and said her father was still alive. Impulsively she put her hand in his for a few steps, then seemed to realize what she had done and withdrew it, blushing.

Lin chuckled happily. He had never met a girl as shy as Edona. Boldly he took her hand and held it, not letting her pull it away. She blushed more. The Indians looked from Edona to Lin knowingly and spoke rapidly to her in their language. She shook her head violently, but smiled in confusion. Lin didn't need to know their language to know what they were saying.

"I don't care if I am dead," he thought.

They came to the foot of a ladder leading to the roof of one of the buildings that hugged the cliff. Edona started up it with an ease that suggested she had been using these ladders for a long time.

Lin followed her, wondering just how long she and her father had been here. It had been six years since he left college. Edona would have been around fifteen then. Had she and her father been here as long as five years? It seemed likely from Edona's shyness toward him. Maybe she wasn't used to being with young American men.

What was the discovery that had brought Dr. Morell and his daughter to this place? It was embodied in the mysterious belt, whatever it was.

Suddenly it occurred to Lin that there could be no reason for Edona not to tell him what it was all about now. On the roof he stopped her as she was about to enter a doorway.

"There's no danger now," he said. "Will you tell me what it's all about now?"

"Not yet," she said. "My father and the others can tell you so much better, and it will only be a little while. We're almost there."

Lin sighed. Edona smiled at the picture of unwilling patience, then ducked her head and went through the doorway.

Lin followed. Edona crossed the room, which was bare of furnishings except for rugs and tapestries. She pulled aside a tapestry hanging on a wall, revealing the opening of a tunnel whose walls were rough stone rather than the adobe-like material of the building.

The tunnel led back perhaps twenty feet, opening into a small room carved out of the solid rock. The walls were very rough.

Edona reached underneath a rough projection near the floor. When she straightened, a section of the wall was moving slowly back. It moved without noise. After it had retreated into the wall two feet it began to rise. In five minutes there was revealed another tunnel, leading on into the mountain.

Lin examined the walls of this tunnel as they went into it. The block of movable stone, from the cracks in the tunnel, was ten feet thick.

"It's balanced with a stone counterweight," Edona explained. "And works by hydraulics. The place where we are going has been used by—a certain hereditary group, for a thousand years."

They were alone in the passage. Lin took Edona's hand. She resisted his hold, embarrassed.

"Please," she said.

"You'd better get used to it," Lin said calmly. He started walking. Edona tried feebly to free her hand, then walked beside him, her head half turned away.

"How long have you been here?" Lin asked to break the silence.

"Almost five years," Edona replied. "We came here when I was fifteen."

"That explains it," Lin said. And Edona didn't ask what it explained. She was walking beside him more easily now. After a hundred yards of unhurried walking, her fingers curled around his hand.

Lin's heart beat faster. He compared Edona with the worldly-wise girls of his experience. They would have considered holding hands childish and silly. Lin couldn't remember a kiss that had made his heart quicken like Edona's fingers curling around his, here in the privacy of this tunnel.

He wondered what it would be like to kiss her. And he was disappointed when the tunnel ended.

CHAPTER THREE

THE PLACE they were in was a large cavern. Its roof curved up to a height of twenty feet. It was at least fifty feet across to the far side. Scattered near the wall were blankets and furs that were probably used for sleeping. Here and there were dark openings that led away from this central room.

In the center of the floor was a fire burning brightly, the smoke rising upward and drifting along the ceiling to be caught by invisible currents and whisked into an opening at the highest point. Forming a half-moon around the fireplace were stacks of wood.

The fire was the only source of illumination Lin could see. There were women working over it, stirring things in kettles suspended over the flames.

The men in this cavern were not Indians. They wore white robes that draped like the robes in pictures Lin had seen of Romans in the days of the Roman Empire. Two of these men had sprung up from beds of rugs and furs as they had entered, and were coming toward them eagerly.

"I see you brought him," one of them said in English.

Edona spoke to him swiftly in a language that was different than the one the Indians had used. He scowled angrily. Lin guessed she had told him about the two men who had pursued her. Now Edona changed to English.

"Lin," she said. "This is Rax Antl." The second man had come up and stood welcoming Lin with a broad grin that formed criss-cross wrinkles in a wide, angry scar that went from his left jaw line up through a vacant left eye into his forehead. "And this is Artaxl," Edona introduced him.

Lin grinned at Artaxl, taking an instinctive liking to him in spite of the evil appearance of his scar. The man's smile was infectious. There was a light of humor and laughter and deep understanding in his right eye.

He pulled his eyes away and sized up Rax Antl, Rax was a serious type. The smile on his face was not habitual. Yet there was something about him that created in Lin a feeling of respect.

"He looks smart," Lin thought as he shook hands with Rax. He guessed that Rax was probably the leader of whatever group centered about this hidden cavern.

Then Lin shook hands with Artaxl, grinning broadly.

"Now maybe I can find out what all this is about," he said.

"Hasn't Edona told you?" Artaxl asked, surprised.

"There wasn't time," Edona said. She added some swift words in the strange language, then apologized to Lin. "They don't know English well enough to explain things quickly."

She turned back to Rax Antl. "My father?" she asked quietly.

Immediately Rax and Artaxl became grave.

"He's much worse," Rax said. "You'd better see him at once."

Edona left them and ran across the cavern to one of the many dark openings. Lin followed her more slowly, Rax and Artaxl keeping beside him.

"What's wrong with him?" Lin asked.

"He was working with the instrument of cold," Rax said.

"A refrigerator?" Lin asked, feeling sure that was not it. Both men laughed shortly at this question.

"No, not a refrigerator," Artaxl said grimly. "A refrigerator merely takes away the energy of heat from an object. The instrument of cold draws in the living cold of empty space and directs it like a force—only you can't always direct it where you will. It turned on him."

"Is that what turned on you?" Lin asked.

"Me?" Artaxl echoed. "Oh." He touched a finger to the broad, livid scar. He smiled mirthlessly. "No. That was a knife, in my younger days when I was more foolhardy and less peaceful than now."

"Tell him the truth," Rax said. "That scar is my life. You could have avoided it—by letting the blade go where it was intended."

"And let Montakotl have the pleasure of destroying his successor?" Artaxl mocked. "I couldn't have done that. I don't regret the scar."

"Neither do I," Rax Antl said softly. "When I see it I know there is one man I can safely turn my back on."

Edona appeared at the mouth of the tunnel and motioned silently for Lin to hurry.

"Father wants to see you," she whispered.

Lin recognized Dr. Morell immediately. There were deep lines of suffering etched on his face. His cheeks were sunken, the eyes blazing with fever; but that high, intellectual forehead and firm mouth would have been recognizable anywhere.

Dr. Morell smiled weakly as Lin entered the small room, and raised an emaciated, pale hand, laced with blue veins. He tried to rise from his position on the bed of furs, but sank back helplessly.

"How do you do, Lin, my boy," he said, his voice; barely above a whisper. "I'm sorry if I've been the cause of yanking you away from something important..."

"Don't let it bother you, sir," Lin said. He looked meaningfully at Edona. "Nothing is more important than what you yanked me into."

Lin's eyes dropped to the clean bandaging on Dr. Morell's side. The man was naked to the waist, his ribs standing out. Above the bandage the skin was an orange yellow, shading into dark blue tinged with green at the very edge of the bandage.

He had never seen gangrene, but he thought that must be what it was. And from the size of the bandage at least a third of

Dr Morell's midsection must be nothing but dead or decaying tissue.

"The cold of outer space," Artaxl had said. What had he meant? Outer space was cold because it contained no matter to hold heat.

"I haven't much time left," Dr. Morell was saying. Edona, a look of suffering in her eyes, dropped beside her father and lifted him so that his head rested in her arms.

"Nonsense," Lin said with a show of confidence. "I'll go back and bring the finest doctor in Los Angeles. He'll be able to fix you up."

"I must explain to you what this is all about," Dr. Morell went on, ignoring Lin's words. "Have you told him anything, Edona?" He looked up at his daughter questioningly.

"There wasn't time, father," Edona said.

"Then I'd better begin at the beginning," Dr. Morell said. He cleared his throat feebly. "About the time you were a student of mine—yes, I think right during that time, I was doing some experiments for the government on the separation of U-235 from U-238. I want to tell you about that because some of the other things Edona and Rax and Artaxl can tell you, but not this. My experiments were along the line of segregation of elements by passing them through a magnetic field so that elements with the same chemical properties but different inertial masses could be separated. Work had already been done in that field; but I was trying a different technique in an attempt to get better results."

"I understand," Lin said quietly. "I read your paper on it two years later."

"Good," Dr. Morell said. "But all my findings weren't in that paper. I was doing all right with my work until I started to use refined Uranium from a new field in Alaska. From the very start the metal acted up. It was slightly magnetic in its own right, for one thing. For another, there was some kind of impurity in it, a metal of some kind, that made its melting point several degrees higher than it should be.

"In the magnetic separator it didn't work at all. The atomic streams would bend sharply. This new element was condensing the Uranium and carrying it with it. Finally I decided to use chemical means to try to get rid of the impurity. I succeeded all right, but then I found that the impurity was something worth experimenting with. To cut a long story short, it was an element higher in the scale than any yet known, and it had most of the properties of iron.

"I was about to make my discovery known when I found out something that made me keep quiet. I found that although the new element had an atomic *mass* higher than Uranium, its atomic *weight* was that of ordinary iron."

"You mean," Lin said. "That in a field it had a measurable inertial mass greater than Uranium, but in a lump it weighed the same as iron?"

"That's right," Dr. Morell agreed. "And altogether I had accumulated almost five pounds of the stuff in my purification of the Uranium sent me from the Alaska refinery. I decided to keep quiet until I had learned more about the stuff. There at the college I couldn't learn much more, though. The college is at a point where there is a high mountain on Earth II."

"Earth II?" Lin asked. "Then that is this world where we are now?"

"No, this is Earth V," Dr. Morell said. "But I'm getting ahead of myself. What I mean is, at the college the stuff couldn't show its property of slipping over into other planes because it can't do so if the substances bordering Earth III there are solid."

He coughed. Then his face contorted with pain. His hand went instinctively to his side covered by the bandage.

"I'm just confusing you," he said. "But there will have to be a little confusion until you understand it all. You won't be any more confused than I was on my vacation."

"You graduated in fifty-three didn't you, Lin?" Dr. Morell asked.

"Yes," Lin answered.

"It was during the summer of fifty-three that Edona and I went to a cabin I own up in the San Bernadino Range. I took the stuff with me. I had melted it and made it into ten-gauge wire for convenience. My first experiment was to use some of it as a core for a small magnet in order to study its magnetic properties more."

Dr. Morell grinned.

"The small magnet simply vanished," he said. "Its wires, connected to a dry cell, hung downward like the rope hangs upward in the Indian rope trick. In my excitement my arm hit the dry cell. It rolled off the table and vanished before it hit the floor. The whole thing had just disappeared.

"That was the start. I used smaller amounts of the stuff, and took great precautions. In a month I had settled on what I firmly believed to be the true explanation of the whole setup. And that's what I want to convey to you. The others can tell you what's going on, and why I sent for you."

"We can explain that to him ourselves, father," Edona said. "You'd better rest now."

"No, I feel strong enough," Dr. Morell said. "You might leave out something vital. Lin, matter has some of the properties of light. With what I learned I conceived matter as being radiant energy traveling at the speed of light in the fourth dimension. If that were so, then all reality as we had known it would be merely a wave front, with each particle a quantum of light, and all actions between particles of matter being interference phenomena. It wasn't a new concept, exactly. But it brought up the possibility of other wave fronts ahead of and behind us, in the fourth dimension.

"An entire world could occupy the same position in three-space as our Earth—and be separated from it by a millionth of an inch in the fourth dimension. The whole universe as it is known to science could be a hyperplane wave-front of almost zero thickness. That seemed, and still seems, to be the answer.

"Anyway, I discovered that summer that there was an Earth whose sea level is about two miles below that of the world I had been taught was the only one. I also discovered there was a third Earth whose sea level was about two miles higher.

"I found that any solid attached to a piece of this strange stuff when it is magnetized to saturation will be dragged along with it into one of these other worlds. It was then that I started to make the belts."

A spasm of coughing shook Dr. Morell's emaciated frame. Specks of blood flecked his lips as he lay spent from the ordeal.

"Let me tell him about that," Edona said. When there was no answer she continued talking, her voice subdued in the atmosphere of death that hovered over her father.

"There was something before the belts," she began. "Father experimented until he could send objects—it was into the second plane, since the surface of Earth V was above the cabin and thus presented a hyperplane wall against any invasion of the fifth plane from Earth III there. He built a cage and sent a frog I caught through. It came back alive and unharmed.

"Then he conceived the idea of sending a camera through and taking a picture. The pictures he took showed a world very much like Earth III—"

"Is Earth III the world we were born on?" Lin interrupted.

"Yes, Lin," Edona said. "You'll see in a while why we call it Earth III. To get back, the pictures showed a world very much like the one we knew—but from an altitude of around ten thousand feet. Maybe more.

"I helped him a lot of the time. Sometimes I took the pictures by myself. For a whole week we did nothing but take pictures, one every half hour. Father kept making refinements. He got the angles down to exact degrees. That way he determined that the new world, Earth II, was co-centric with Earth III.

"We used filters and took shots of the sun of Earth II and found that it was co-centric with Sun III, but one and twenty-four hundredths times as bright. We found that Moon II was co-centric with Moon III and measurably smaller.

"We sent thermometers through and found the temperature colder. We took all sorts of measurements. Father built a freeze spring scale and found objects weighed less in the gravity field of Earth II. The air pressure was about the same on both sides. We know now that the reason for that is inter-plane leakage, but then, of course, we didn't know anything. We were just experimenting to find out.

"All the time father was educating me on four-dimensional geometry. He showed me how *a solid object presents every part of its interior directly to the fourth dimension, so that a three dimensional solid is in reality a hyperplane of no thickness.*"

"Yes," Lin interrupted. "I understand all that. Go on with the experiments."

"Father wanted to go over into this other world himself," Edona continued. "The trouble was, how could he get back if he did? The only answer was an airplane fitted up with the inter-plane field unit. The pictures had shown a large flat field that would make a good landing field, and father had had lessons in flying so that he felt he could go there and return without trouble.

"So, two months after the discovery of Earth II we started concentrating on the problem of flying into the second earth-plane. There were a lot of ifs. We could if the inter-plane field would take the plane across. We could if the gasoline in the gas tank would come too. We could if we were carried across too."

Edona laughed lightly at the memory of all the worries they had had.

"We found a farmer near San Bernadino who was willing to let us bring a plane there and use one of his fields for a landing field. We built the large inter-plane unit right into the cockpit. Then we took off.

"We weren't too sure of the topography of Earth III right there, so father decided to climb as high as he could before turning on the inter-plane field. That way, he could be sure of time to adjust to the new conditions whatever they might turn out to be."

"But I had overlooked one little detail," Dr. Morell spoke up, smiling sadly.

"Yes," Edona smiled. "Like the crook in the story, he had overlooked one thing. He realized it instantly when we kicked out of the third Earth-plane, though. But it was too late."

She shuddered.

"I still wake up at night when I dream about it," she said. "Father threw in the switch on the plane—oh yes, I forgot about the belts. They were a precaution at the time. Father wasn't sure the plane would take us along. We were wearing the belts and parachutes just in case it didn't. It did, though. And the first thing we saw as the plane went across was a big tree right ahead of us. There wasn't time to get out of its way. A wing hit it and fell off. Then we were crashing through branches. We landed with a big bounce. I think I was knocked out for a minute, but I'm not sure.

"Anyway, we landed all in one piece physically—just three or four miles from this very spot where we are now."

"You see," Dr. Morell spoke up. "I hadn't considered the possibility of there being still another Earth. We rose above its surface when we went up in the plane. When I turned on the inter-plane field, *the greater gravity of Earth V pulled us this way instead of into the second Earth-plane.*"

"What about Earth four?" Lin asked. "Or is there one?"

"There's where the Inca science comes in," Edona said.

"Inca?" Lin echoed. "Then—"

He looked questioningly at Artaxl and Rax.

CHAPTER FOUR

"YES," Artaxl said. "We're descendants of the Incas of South America. Our ancestors had known of heavy-iron for a long time. We lived in both worlds, entering through a doorway that used the same principle Dr. Morell discovered, at a spot where the surfaces of both Earths met, high in the Andes."

"Whew!" Lin said, taking out his handkerchief and mopping his forehead. "Now I've heard everything." He grinned at a sudden thought. "I suppose you took all the fabulous tons of gold with you too," he said. Artaxl and Rax nodded. "But your white skin," Lin objected. "The Incas were Indian-like those people I met out in the village."

"The Incas were always two races," Artaxl said. "One white, the other red. I don't believe the Spaniards got to see any of the white ones."

Lin shook his head in amazement.

"Don't ask me the origin of either race," Artaxl said with dry amusement. "No one knows for sure, though legend has it that both races came from the Moon in two log canoes. One got caught in a whirlpool and drifted too close to the sun, getting burnt a fiery red before they could escape and rejoin their fellow pioneers. There are half a dozen other legends to account for the two races. One is that God created man from corn, and since there is red corn and white corn, man had two colors."

Dr. Morell raised his head.

"I'd like to be alone with Lin for a minute," he said with great dignity. "Then I would like to rest."

Edona's lips trembled as she rose to leave. Artaxl put his arm around her shoulders and led her out, followed by Rax. When they were gone Lin squatted down by Dr. Morell.

"I'm not going to live much longer, Lin," Dr. Morell said. "There's so much I should tell you; but I haven't the strength. Rax will tell you of the big danger facing us, that you must find the answer to."

"The cold?" Lin asked.

"No, not that," Dr. Morell said. "That's no danger if you leave it alone. In the sixth Earth-plane there's no planet. Only a great Sargasso Sea of things better left alone. They're held there by the time-dense spread of the gravity fields of the four Earths. There's no danger there—unless Montakotl uses his weapons— dares to risk using them."

Lin remained silent, waiting for Dr. Morell to say what he wanted to say without explaining.

"Things are going to happen fast," Dr. Morell went on weakly. "You'll learn what they are. Whatever their outcome, I want you to take care of Edona, see that she's not left alone to the mercies of an unbelieving world or an alien world, whichever it is to be."

"Of course I will," Lin said. He smiled into Dr. Morell's burning eyes. "I had ideas about doing that even before I came here."

Dr. Morell returned his smile. Suddenly the feverish fire in his eyes seemed to go out. For a minute Lin thought he had died; but the gaunt chest of the dying man still moved rhythmically.

"Are you all right?" Lin asked.

There was no answer. Lin waited another minute, then rose quietly and left. An Indian woman was standing in the short passageway to the large cave. She let Lin pass her and then went in to tend to Dr. Morell.

Edona was sitting on the stone floor to the right of the opening as Lin stepped into the cavern. Her back was against the wall, her arms locked over her knees, a forlorn expression on her face.

Lin bent over and lifted her to her feet. For a moment she was close, her lips scant inches from his, her eyes large and wistful.

"Come over and get something to eat," Artaxl's voice boomed.

The spell was broken. Edona stepped away.

"You must be hungry," she said. "And I'll have to eat whether I'm hungry or not—or the Indian women will hover around me all evening worrying about my health."

Lin reached out to take her hand in an attempt to regain the moment he had lost. Edona eluded his grasp and ran smiling across the cavern to where Artaxl was holding two plates of steaming food.

She took one. Her eyes teased Lin as he came up and Artaxl thrust the other plate in his hands. Lin glared at her with mock anger. Artaxl missed nothing. His one eye twinkled as he accepted a third plate from one of the Indian women.

Acting as host, he led Lin and Edona to a large rug of bright colors in Indian designs. He sat down cross-legged. When Edona did the same, Lin sat down with his legs out straight.

"Can't you cross your legs?" Artaxl asked.

Lin tried it. Edona and Artaxl laughed at the ungainly position he assumed. Lin laid his plate on the rug and stretched out full length, propping his head on one elbow.

"This is more comfortable," he said.

"Bad etiquette here," Artaxl said tolerantly. "It's a good thing there aren't any youngsters in here. They would get spanked just for watching you eat that way."

Lin's eyes roamed over the cavern. Suddenly he sat up in surprise. Across the cavern was Rax Antl. With him was a woman. Tall, her skin was white. Her long hair covering her shoulders was jet black. Her features were almost too perfect. Her eyes, even across the distance of thirty or forty feet that separated her from Lin, were large and filled with some strange magnetism. They were watching Lin. They locked with his. Her red lips smiled slowly.

"Who's that?" Lin asked. Artaxl followed Lin's gaze.

"That's Mara," he said gruffly. "She's Rax's wife. Beware, of her. Her sport is to make men fall in love with her, and flaunt their love in Rax's face."

"I take it you don't like her," Lin said lightly.

Artaxl's eye turned on Lin coldly. For a minute Lin withstood its fury. He sensed that this white descendant of the Incas could and probably had killed men while that cold hate flared in him. He decided to be a little more careful of what he said.

Rax and Mara were crossing over to them leisurely, talking to each other. Mara's white robe, of some texture more yielding than that of the robes worn by the men, revealed the rounded contours of her graceful body. Lin sensed she was conscious of this and was looking for some sign of its effect on him.

He turned his eyes to Edona who was watching him, a strained expression on her face. He smiled at her reassuringly, looked back at the approaching Mara with his expression politely impersonal.

A slight frown of anger flitted over Mara's face, then she was smiling again. Rax seemed unaware of this undercurrent. As he and Mara stopped at the edge of the rug Artaxl rose. Lin followed suit, standing awkwardly, ill at ease.

"My wife Mara, Lin Carter," Rax said, a note of pride in his voice.

"How do you do, Lin," Mara said. She smiled down at Edona with condescending superiority. "Edona has taught us our English very well, don't you think?"

"Quite well," Lin said, matching her tones. "You could pass for one of us back on Earth III—almost."

Edona's and Artaxl's eyes flashed admiration at this thrust. Mara's nostrils flared delicately as the only indication that she had felt it. Only Rax remained oblivious of it.

"I wonder how I would look in a dress," Mara said, looking down at Edona speculatively. "Perhaps if you saw me in one, Lin Carter, you would retract that—almost."

She took a studied breath that revealed her high pointed breasts to full advantage under the loose robe. Lin dropped his gaze hastily, conscious of Edona's eyes on him.

Mara sat down on the rug. The three men settled themselves. Lin returned to his food. It was a sort of vegetable stew with large chunks of gamey meat in it, giving it a rich flavor that was extremely satisfying.

"What kind of meat is this?" Lin asked conversationally.

"A quotl," Edona replied. "The same as that animal that crashed through the underbrush on our way here."

"Oh," Lin said lamely. He was conscious of Mara watching him with studious eyes, probing him. There was a silence.

"What is this threat hanging over you?" Lin asked. "Dr. Morell said you would tell me. He didn't have the strength to tell me much after you left."

"He didn't tell you about the minor planet?" Rax asked. "I thought that was what he wanted to talk to you alone about."

"What about the minor planet?" Lin asked.

"I'll tell him," Artaxl said to the others.

"It's a small planet on the fifth Earth-plane," he began. "It's had a regular orbit ever since our astronomers were able to understand the mathematics of astronomy and figure such things. A year ago something happened to it. Maybe it was hit by a wandering body when no one was looking. It changed its course, so now it's going to strike Earth V—unless. And that unless will be bad news for Earth III. There's only one way to avoid its hitting Earth V and probably destroying all life here. The thing's two hundred miles in diameter and will probably crack whatever planet it hits wide open, releasing its internal fires, in addition to the heat of its fall.

"That way is to build an inter-plane field right on the approaching body and shift it into another time-plane."

"How can that threaten Earth III?" Lin asked. "You can kick it into the sixth plane where there is no Earth for it to strike, can't you?"

"You don't quite understand the nature of inter-plane travel yet," Artaxl said, frowning. "Basically it amounts to this: *the field generated by the heavy-iron core isn't exactly a drive field. It's a null-grav field, tight in the plane in which it exists, but open in the fourth dimension.* As soon as it goes on, *the gravity field* of the other planes pulls on the field and everything in its influence, and *draws it in whatever direction, forward or backwards, that gravity is strongest,* assuming there is no dense matter in either direction of the fourth dimension to block it.

"In order to make it jump out of the fifth plane, the inter-plane field must be turned on as it approaches us. Then it will be drawn in the only direction where there is another strong gravitational field—Earth III, your own world."

"You can't do that," Lin said, unbelieving. "That would destroy billions of human beings."

"We agree with you," Artaxl said grimly. "That's why we're with Dr. Morell. But Montakotl thinks differently. He doesn't feel any responsibility for human life on Earth III. He's determined to go ahead with his plan to save Earth V. In fact, he thinks it's a God-given chance to even the score with the Conquistadors for driving our ancestors out of South America."

"But none of you agree with him, I hope?" Lin asked, looking from one face to another.

"Certainly not," Rax Antl said firmly. "There are perhaps three million of us altogether. We don't believe the billions of Earth III should be sacrificed to save our three millions. Anyway, it wouldn't mean our destruction. Every one of us has a belt similar to the one you are wearing. At the very last second we could all jump to Earth III."

Lin blinked his eyes, then chuckled.

"I was just forming a mental picture of three million people parachuting into California out of a clear sky," he explained. "The Los Angeles Chamber of Commerce would go insane." He sobered at their blank looks. They had missed the point of his joke. "But is that all the people on Earth V?" He asked. "How come? It's a bigger Earth than Earth III, with all its billions."

"There are billions here," Rax said. "The scientific method isn't something they accept. None of them take to civilization. Very few of them have a written language, and most tribes and small nations are suspicious of all others, and kill strangers without waiting to find out what they want."

"Of course there may be places on the other side of Earth V that are civilized," Artaxl cut in. "If so, they haven't discovered inter-plane travel nor space travel, or we would have met up with them in our own space travels."

"You haven't flown around to the other side to find out?" Lin asked.

"That would take power we don't have," Artaxl said. "I'll explain how we travel in space without using power. We kick our ships into the Earth III plane. They start to fall. Your atmosphere catches them and gives them a chance to gain speed by a long glide. Just before they are about to hit the ground they're kicked into the Earth II plane. That gives them another couple of miles to gain speed in their long glide. Then they're kicked over into the Earth I plane.

"Earth I is only a couple of hundred miles in diameter itself. It has no atmosphere; but by timing things right the ship can use its weak gravitational field to gain direction, and it already has escape velocity from Earth I."

"I get the idea," Lin said thoughtfully. "Then, in space it can use charts to get into the vicinity of a body in any plane and kick into its plane the same way."

"That's right," Artaxl agreed.

"But back to this approaching planetoid," Lin said. "Wouldn't it take quite a big field to kick such a huge thing into another plane?"

"It would take a core of about thirty tons of heavy iron," Rax said.

"Where would they get all that?" Lin asked.

"We have thousands of tons of it," Rax said. "You see, we've been collecting it a long time. We mine it from Earth III by a very simple process. Our mines are about two miles under the surface. Our mining machines grind the ore up into fine powder. The powder is run through a field that kicks the heavy-iron granules into hoppers on Earth II. Those granules run about fifty percent pure heavy-iron. We could mine a hundred tons a day if we needed to."

"Nothing can surprise me any more," Lin said. "That did it. Descendants of the Incas on Earth V mining for an element unknown to science in mines two miles under the surface in Earth III, with the refined ore falling into hoppers on Earth II. Spaceships that get away from the Earth by falling down. This morning I suspected I was crazy when two men ran into my room, pulled the ripcords of their parachutes, and sank through my rug without disturbing the dust on it."

"Those were Montakotl's men," Rax said darkly. "He knows you're here by now, and will have his spies looking for you."

"I want to get this straight," Lin said. "With the inter-plane or null-grav field on this planetoid it will pull or fall into the Earth III plane. Why won't it go over into the Earth II plane just as easily? Then nobody would be hurt."

"It couldn't do that until its bulk was blocked from the Earth V plane by the solid mass of Earth V," Edona explained. "And that's impossible, since Earth V's bulk only sticks up a couple of miles over Earth III."

"Well," Lin said, frowning in concentration. "When it gets into the Earth III plane, what's to keep it from jumping back into the Earth V plane? Some kind of cutout that shuts off the power when the shift to the third plane is accomplished?"

"That's right," Rax spoke up.

"It looks like a choice between two evils," Lin said seriously. "Nature presented Montakotl with a choice of killing his own three million people—or killing a couple of billion other human beings, disregarding the ones we don't know much about here on Earth V."

"And he chose to save his own," Mara said.

"How soon is this body going to strike?" Lin asked grimly.

"Very soon now," Artaxl said. He dropped his eyes to the rug. Rax and Mara also looked away. They believed, Lin sensed, that Montakotl would succeed, that the Earth Lin had been born on, together with all its people, would be destroyed.

Only Edona looked at him. In her eyes were a confidence and a belief that because her father had called Lin, he could avert disaster. But could he? Sickeningly, he realized that he hadn't one single idea of what to do.

"WOULD YOU like to see the moon?" Edona asked Lin as he finished his food and laid the plate on top of her and Artaxl's empty ones at the edge of the rug. Lin looked at her blankly.

"Of course," he exclaimed, "I would like to see it. It isn't the same moon."

"There's a ledge far up the cliff looking out over the valley where we can see for miles," Edona said.

Lin looked at Artaxl and Rax.

"Go ahead," Artaxl said. "We can send for you if—if anything requires it."

"Maybe we'll join you later," Mara said. Artaxl glared at her and shook his head imperceptibly. She smiled sweetly at him with her lips.

Edona took Lin's hand with brave possessiveness and led him away. They were both conscious of Mara's eyes following them. Edona walked close to Lin as they crossed the cavern to one of the many dark openings. But when they had entered the tunnel and were alone, she gently withdrew her hand.

"So that was just for Mara's benefit," Lin growled.

"Oh no," Edona said, turning innocent eyes up at him.

"So you did it because you like to have me hold your hand then?" Lin smiled.

"No!" Edona exclaimed. "That is, I—" A spark of genius rose to her rescue. "What did you and father talk about when you were alone?" she asked in an attempt to change the subject.

"We talked about you," Lin said, sensing the objective of the question and knowing it had failed.

"Oh," Edona said lamely.

Without warning Lin took her head in his hands and held her face in front of his. He didn't try to kiss her, but just held her there, waiting.

Her hands came up and tried to pull his away. She tried ineffectively to twist loose from his grasp. Her eyes flashed fire at him. Then, slowly, her hands dropped away. The defiance and protest in her eyes died down. Not until then did he kiss her.

Her hand, which he had held with unyielding strength, rested lightly between the palms of his hands. Her lips surrendered hesitantly, then fiercely. He felt her body touching his.

His arms went around her and drew her close. He felt her arms creep around his shoulders. Abruptly her lips pulled away. She buried her head against his neck, her arms holding tight with constricting strength.

Amazedly Lin realized she was crying. She was weeping silently.

"Here now," he growled softly. His hand came up and pressed against her soft hair.

"I can't help it," Edona whispered in his neck.

"Of course you can't," Lin said. "And who else's shoulder can you cry on?" His voice took on a note of grave gaiety. "Don't let me ever catch you crying on someone else's shoulder."

Her sobs changed to a subdued laugh. She pulled away from him, looking away in embarrassment.

He caught her hand and held it. Then they were walking along the tunnel side by side, intimately silent.

The tunnel went upward, twisting back on itself every fifty yards. There were marks of cutting tools on the granite walls. Lin wondered how long it had taken the natives to cut this tunnel. Had they used machine borers? Or had they whittled away at the hard stone, taking years to accomplish their task?

Something Mara had said came into his mind. She had said Edona had done a good job of teaching them English. There was another sign of the passage of time. Five years during which Edona had lived here, two miles straight up from Los Angeles, staying with her father so he wouldn't be alone, occupying her time by teaching the people here to speak her language—and incidentally learning to speak their languages.

The ledge they came to was high up on the face of the cliff. It was night. Below spread the darkness of the forest, half lit by a bright red moon.

The moon was low on the horizon to the east. Lin was surprised at its smallness, less than half the diameter of the moon of his own Earth. But its most unusual aspect was its redness.

Even the feeble light it sent into the shadows of the landscape below were reddish, so that the scene was one of eerie study in deep reds and blacks.

To one side on the ledge there was a vague movement. It was an Indian sentinel, watching for any signs of movement below on the approaches to the village. He looked up at them, then resumed his watch, ignoring them.

Edona sat down. Lin sat near her, finding that there was one of the ever present rugs on the stone floor of the ledge.

"Moon V is about fifty thousand miles farther away than Moon III," Edona said quietly. "The most remarkable thing about it to my way of thinking is that it always remains directly behind Moon III. Their periods are exactly the same. Sometimes it's very close to Moon III, because the eccentricity of its orbit is greater."

"How do they account for its staying behind Moon III?" Lin asked. "Do they suspect some connection between the two moons?"

"There may have been originally," Edona said. "You see, gravity is a plane-dense field. The Incas and father have it all worked out mathematically. Matter in adjacent planes has little effect on matter in any plane; but with aggregates as large as the Earth their separate gravity fields work on each other like a sort of fluid drive mechanism. That inter-planar action holds the four Earths concentric and keeps them rotating at the same rate.

"With Moon III and Moon V, if they were originally eccentric, one of them was in an unnatural orbit, or maybe both of them in some sort of compromise orbit. But the fourth dimensional attraction between them was very weak, and eventually they pulled apart, each taking up an orbit consistent with the gravity of its own plane."

"You knew," Lin said thoughtfully. "Maybe more is known about this on Earth III than most people suspect. I seem to remember reading someplace about a dark moon hidden behind the regular moon."

"Would you like to see the other moon?" Edona asked.

She got to her feet and went over to the Indian. She spoke to him in a low voice, returning with something in her hand. It was a glass disc about four inches in diameter and almost an inch thick.

She held it up to Lin's eyes. Through it he could see the familiar Moon of his own Earth, pale and unreal like it sometimes appears in broad daylight in the sky. It was superimposed over the smaller red moon of Earth V.

"That reminds me," Lin said. "What about Earth IV? Is there one?"

"The Incas say there is," Edona said. "They say it's small, and that because it's small, the greater gravity fields of Earth V and Earth III make things jump across rather than stopping in the fourth plane. They tell lots of interesting stories of Earth IV. No matter how fantastic they are, no one can dispute them, because there's no way of getting there to find out. But even they don't believe what they say. So far as anyone really knows, there's only the four planes of Earth."

"Maybe the ancients knew about them," Lin said. "They talked about the four elements of Earth, the four corners of the Earth, and lots of other mysterious fours."

"Seven is another mysterious number," Edona said. "The Incas insist there are seven Suns, and seven planes to the solar system, with planets on all seven planes. They claim their spaceships have gone into all seven planes and mapped the complete solar system, but those charts aren't here. They're in the Inca capital city, Montaca."

"That's what I like about you," Lin said. "You spring things on me so casually. Ever since you handed me that belt and dropped out of sight through the rug without telling me what it was about."

"I'm sorry," Edona said with real contriteness. "But it's so hard not to. Montaca is a large city, the only one I know of on Earth V. I've seen it, though I've never been right in it. I think it's ugly."

"Where is it?" Lin asked. Edona pointed south along the cliff base of the mountain.

"It's that way," she said. "About ten miles from here. You could see it except for the fact that the cliffs block the view. The spaceport is just south of it."

The Indian at the other end of the ledge spoke softly in his short, chopped tongue. Edona replied in the same language.

"He said one of our spies came from the direction of Montaca just before we arrived here on the ledge," she translated. "He says that now the sounds of feet approach here. He thinks it's Artaxl, and that Artaxl is in a hurry."

Lin listened.

"I don't hear anything," he said. "Does he have some kind of listening device?"

"No," Edona said. "The lookouts are chosen because of their keen senses. They can see in the dark, and hear things that aren't audible to ordinary hearing."

The Indian's prediction was born out at once. A shadowy figure emerged from the tunnel mouth and dropped down beside Edona and Lin with a grunt. It was Artaxl.

"A spy came from Montaca," he said briefly. "He reports that the inter-plane drive for the planetoid is being loaded to take out into space. By this time, he says, it's on board the spaceship. That means that as soon as Earth V swings around to the point where the ship can take off and head toward the planetoid it will start."

"How long will that be?" Lin asked.

"Some time tomorrow afternoon," Artaxl replied.

Lin stared out over the dark valley thoughtfully.

"Would there be a chance of stealing the ship?" he asked.

"We could try it," Artaxl said. "I doubt if it would be too heavily guarded for a surprise assault. They could follow and recapture it, but then it might be too late for them to set up the drive on the planetoid."

He sounded reluctant.

"What's the matter with that plan?" Lin asked. "Do you know of any other way to stop Montakotl from wrecking Earth III?"

"No," Artaxl said quickly. "It's the only plan open to us. We must make it succeed at all costs."

"Let's go down and get the men together and talk it over," Lin suggested.

They stood up. Artaxl stood there for a moment, the vague outlines of his body motionless as if he were discussing something within himself. Edona's hand searched for and found Lin's in the darkness.

Then Artaxl turned and vanished into the tunnel.

Lin and Edona followed, walking swiftly on the downslope of the tunnel floor.

When they entered the main cavern they saw Rax and several men, both Indian and white Incas, in a group to one side. Mara was there, standing aloof near by.

They saw them, and stopped talking, waiting for them to join the group. Artaxl went ahead. When Lin got within earshot Artaxl was talking earnestly in the Inca language to the others.

"I was telling them of your plan to steal the ship," he explained.

"The best time to try it," Rax spoke up, "is at dawn. We will have to start in five hours if we are to get there in time to do that."

"I wish we had guns," Lin said.

"Guns would be no good against the weapons of Montakotl," Artaxl said. "Our only hope of success is complete surprise."

"What are these weapons of Montakotl?" Lin asked. "They must be something if guns wouldn't help us."

"They are weapons of the cold," Rax said. "Handed down from ancient times. They are so horrible even Montakotl would hesitate to use them; but to save the ship he would."

"That was what Dr. Morell was experimenting on, wasn't it?" Lin asked.

"Yes," Rax replied. "He wanted to understand how they worked. He found out," he added grimly.

"It's settled then that we will attack at dawn," one of the other white Incas said. "We had better sleep so we can be strong and quick."

Lin noticed Artaxl's eye flash in alarm. He followed the direction of his gaze.

Mara was moving away from the group toward one of the dark openings.

"Where are you going, Mara?" Artaxl called.

"Why, to my quarters," Mara said, stopping.

"Your quarters are not in that direction," Artaxl said.

"I choose to have a breath of fresh air before retiring," Mara said frigidly.

She continued on, and vanished through the opening leading to the village at the base of the cliff. Artaxl watched her go, anger suffusing his face. Lin saw that some of the other white Incas were also watching her departure with dark gazes.

Rax Antl didn't seem to be aware of this disturbing current of suspicion—for that was what it truly was. But suspicious of what? Was it possible that Mara might be a spy of Montakotl and might find some way to get word to him that Rax's men were planning to attack the ship waiting to take off for the asteroid? Even Edona was worried about Mara's going out to the village.

Artaxl said something that made it certain none of these people trusted Mara except her own husband.

"I've been thinking," he said. "If we attack an hour before dawn we will have the advantage of darkness with us."

There were quick murmurs of approval. Even Rax seemed very happy about the change. Lin noticed this, and wondered if perhaps Rax might not suspect his wife more than he let on.

"Then we had better get some sleep," Artaxl said. "Lin, you will bunk with me tonight."

CHAPTER SIX

"OF WHAT did you and Dr. Morell speak when you were alone?" Artaxl asked when he and Lin were alone in his room. Lin looked sharply at him. It was on the point of his tongue to tell him that if Dr. Morell had wanted him to know he would have asked him to stay. There was only kindness and friendship on Artaxl's face, not curiosity.

"He asked me to make sure Edona gets safely back home on Earth III when this is over," Lin said simply.

"Yes," Artaxl said with quiet satisfaction. "I had thought that would be it. But was there nothing more?"

"He spoke of the cold," Lin answered. "He said several times that there would be no danger there if I left it alone. But he spoke of a great Sargasso Sea of things in the sixth plane, held there by the hyper-dense spread of the gravity fields of the four Earths. I didn't understand what he meant by that. He said or implied that a great danger lay there if Montakotl used his weapons. What sort of things could they be?"

Artaxl's face had become a mask as Lin spoke. He lay down on his bed of rugs and furs, cupping his head in his hands, his eye hidden from Lin by the bridge of his nose.

"No one knows," he said, his voice strained. "Perhaps they are nothing. Some think they are the primal elements of life, that all life came from the breakthrough of these things into the planes of matter, where they clothed themselves with atoms. Some say they are banished souls. Brave men turn into cowards at the very thought of them, whatever they are. And whatever they are, they are sentient, and hungry.

"The weapon? It's merely a variation of the inter-plane drive, able to reach into another plane and allow anything from that plane to come through. Nature discovered the weapon first. She formed gateways between the worlds with Her discovery. It was through one of them that my ancestors came into Earth V, rather than from any discovery of their own."

He turned on his side, his eye looking piercingly at Lin.

"I have a feeling that before another day is past you will have no more desire to be curious about these things," he said. "In my mind is a prophetic vision of the beings of the cold enwrapping me, sinking into me, taking me for their own—and of many others of them whistling with the winds of space as they come through, loosed by Montakotl's weapons in the hands of crazed men."

"Nonsense," Lin said.

"To you, maybe," Artaxl said. "But not to me. I know. But also I have a prophetic vision of you wresting victory from defeat. In my mind a strange voice whispers, and its whispers are the frigid voice of naked space, from the lips of the Mother of matter. There will be an instant when I will be helpless, and you can save me. When that instant comes you must turn away from me and leave me to my fate, or you will save me only to destroy all mankind. You must promise. You must give me your word that when I tell you to leave me you will obey me."

"I can't give any such promise," Lin said uncomfortably. "And anyway, all this is a lot of nonsense. No one can know the future."

Artaxl's features slowly relaxed. When he spoke again his voice was almost light.

"Then at least remember my words," he said. "And if a time should come when I'm hurt, and you could save my life by risking everything, remember them and act wisely."

"All right," Lin said, having the uncomfortable feeling that Artaxl wasn't as civilized as he had thought, but full of strange beliefs.

That was something he hadn't thought of. These white Incas were still the descendants of a strange race, and not Americans of the twentieth century. They spoke in the correct English Edona had taught them. They behaved and reacted much like ordinary people. But deep down underneath they were filled with the traditions and beliefs of their ancestors.

The atmosphere of the room had become uncomfortable. Lin felt the strong desire to change the subject and get things back on a more rational plane.

"I gathered that you don't trust Mara, Artaxl," he said abruptly. "Why?"

"She's Montakotl's half sister," Artaxl said. "But aside from that, she's not the type who would willingly sacrifice her life to save people she has no interest in. Although she pretends to play along with us, I think she does so merely to be able to hear our plans and relay them to Montakotl, so that Earth V will be safe for her. If she were not Rax's wife—but enough of this. We must sleep."

It seemed only a moment later that Lin felt a gentle hand on his shoulder and woke to see Artaxl's face bending over him.

"Wake up, Lin," he said.

Lin blinked up at the scarred face with its one bright eye. The memory of events flooded into his mind. He stood up and followed Artaxl to the main cavern. The others were already there.

Edona appeared from the direction of her father's room. When she saw Lin she ran to him. He caught her in his arms and held her close while she sobbed, heartbroken. Her father had died during the night while they were asleep.

Artaxl stood by for a moment, then pulled Edona from Lin's arms. He shook her.

"You must take it like a man," he said. "Your grief can come later when there's time. Right now the safety of your world depends on us."

His words sank in. Edona straightened her head and got control of herself.

"You're right, Artaxl," she said. "But now—I'm going with you and Lin."

"Good!" Artaxl said. "It's as the vision said it should be." He glanced at Lin and grinned at him. "We must eat," he said, releasing Edona's shoulders.

After a hasty breakfast of a hot mush that Lin didn't like without cream to sweeten it, they were ready to start.

Rax, his face white and grim, led the way. Artaxl walked with Rax as they went through the tunnel to the village. As they dropped down the ladder to the ground and started along the cliff base to the outer valley he dropped back and whispered to Lin.

"Rax had to tie Mara up," he said. "When she learned we had advanced our plans an hour she was furious. If we get back alive he plans to deal with her."

Tall, muscular Indians from the village had joined the party. There were well over a hundred men, strung out, walking at a swift, distance-eating pace. Here and there along the line were flashlights that cast enough light to enable them to see the path.

When they reached the mouth of the ravine these lights were shut off. They went along in almost total darkness, guided by the shadowy figures in front of them.

In an hour they came to the top of a low hill. Before them stretched the city of Montaca, its outlines revealed by the lights of dozens of open fires distributed through it. Even in the half light the city was ugly, its buildings squat and ungainly.

The leaders of the party took a path that skirted the city while staying within sight of it. It took another hour to get around the acres of sprawled out buildings. Much of the way was through tilled fields and past dark farm dwellings. Lin wondered why dogs didn't bark. He asked Edona about this. She told him dogs were unknown here.

More than once they crossed paved roads in the darkness. Finally they stayed on one of these that led away from the city. Now the way was wide. Edona walked beside Lin.

There was a faint, rosy glow on the eastern horizon when they reached the end of a flat field at least a mile across. In the center of this field, reflecting back the light of the stars, was a gigantic sphere of metal.

The sphere rested in a depression in the earth that made it seem cut off just below the center. And around the sphere was a giant disc of metal that hovered just above the ground like a canopy.

"That sphere is the ship?" Lin asked Artaxl who had dropped back again to be with them.

"No," Artaxl said. "The ship is around the sphere. That sphere is the container for the inter-plane drive unit that is supposed to kick the planetoid into the third plane. Such spheres are often used to carry loads. They can be jettisoned from the ship easily, and also they can be dropped without the ship having to land. Cargo is stored in a central sphere protected by shock springs that will protect it against damage even by a fall from outer space."

Now figures were moving silently away into the darkness. Rax was moving from man to man, whispering commands. The plan seemed to be to completely surround the ship and attack it from all sides.

It would spread their forces out thinly, but would have the advantage of keeping the defenders occupied separately and not give them a chance to get together.

Rax paused long enough to tell Lin he and Edona were to wait until the attack was well under way before attempting to move in and board the ship.

"You can't be of much use to us, Lin," he said. "You have no experience in our type of hand-to-hand fighting. Your job will come after we get possession of the ship. Then your engineering training will be what we will depend on to find a solution to our problems."

"Of course," Lin said. But in his thoughts he was full of doubts. How could his engineering training help him in this? He was less than the most ignorant beginner. The very basics of science involved in space flight and inter-plane travel were unknown to him except in rough outline as he had heard them talking during the past eighteen or twenty hours.

Nevertheless, he agreed heartily that he wouldn't be of much use in the initial attack. These Incas were strong and quick. And his own skill at boxing and wrestling was almost nil.

"Artaxl," Rax said before moving on. "Your job will be to stick with Lin and Edona and protect them if they are attacked."

Artaxl replied in the Inca tongue. Whatever he said caused Rax to smile briefly, and Edona to chuckle. Then he had gone into the night.

Lin, Edona, and Artaxl were alone at the edge of the field, waiting, their bodies lying prone, their heads raised so they could watch for the first sign of action.

When it came it was a scream, chopped off in the middle. That scream was the signal for pandemonium to break loose. Before its echoes died down there was movement in dozens of spots between them and the ship.

"Let's start," Artaxl said gruffly.

He rose to a crouch, leading the way. He was moving into the rosy blush that suffused the eastern horizon. The ship and its center sphere were an unreal prop stuck in the center of an alien scene, to Lin's eyes.

But now something new burst upon the scene, adding to its unreality. It was a blue glow that flashed into being to one side of the ship. It was like a blue light seen through the transparent depths of ice. And accompanying it was the chill sound of glacial winds whistling in alpine mountain clefts.

A blast of air swept past, congealing the perspiration on Lin's skin. He shivered at its touch, and felt its icy tentacles go into him in an unnatural way that no cold he had ever experienced before had done.

Was there a negative energy that was the dynamic opposite of heat? If there was, this was it.

Artaxl muttered words in his own tongue. He had stopped, his head turned upward in an intent stare.

Lin looked up. In the air above there seemed to be vague, gray shadows, spiraling swiftly, appearing out of nothing and vanishing again.

On the field other blue lights had sprung up. On every side sounded screams of fear and agony.

"We must run for it," Artaxl grunted.

He rose from his crouch and ran, Lin and Edona behind him. He glanced over his shoulder every few steps to make sure they were with him.

A figure rose in their path. There was a swift blow of Artaxl's fist and the figure dropped to one side. They brushed past it, going on toward the ship.

There were others ahead of them, climbing the steep ramp that led into the dimly lit interior of the ship.

They reached the ramp and started up. Over their heads suddenly materialized three snake-like shadows of transparent gray. A whining shrill emanated from them. It was both sound and energy, alien in texture.

The things were dropping down. Artaxl knocked Lin and Edona to their knees and stood over them protectively. A fear such as Lin had never experienced possessed him.

The three weaving spirals of icy gray wrapped and twined into Artaxl's flailing arms. They settled over his head. They seemed to soak slowly into his head and hair, to sink in until they were evilly blended with him, seething within him just under the surface of his skin.

"Get into the ship," Artaxl ordered. "Leave me. There's nothing you can do for me. Go."

Lin stood up. He reached toward Artaxl. Artaxl drew back.

"Go!" he screamed. "Go, you fool! Would you destroy your race to save me when nothing can help me?"

Lin hesitated. Suddenly his fist shot out and contacted Artaxl's chin. Even in that brief contact there was a chill that sent horror through Lin's being.

"Help me," he said to Edona.

He took Artaxl's feet and dragged him up the incline, Edona helping him along.

They reached the end of the incline and fell down a short ladder to a metal floor. Figures swept past them up the ladder. There was a clang of banging metal as the hatch cover dropped into place.

Then there was no sound except the tortured moans of Artaxl, no movement but the unholy writhing within his body. And from him was radiating waves of cold that changed perspiration to white frost.

CHAPTER SEVEN

TIME HAD NO MEANING as Lin and Edona crouched over Artaxl in horror, their eyes watching him. He was changing. The moisture of the air was freezing into frost on his skin and flaking off as he writhed in convulsive agony.

His solitary eye was glaring at Lin in hate and accusation. Lin drew back under that glare. Edona drew close to Lin in fear.

"Don't you know what you have done?" Artaxl groaned. "When these things have done with me they will leave me and search for other prey. But there's still time. Drag me to an empty compartment and lock me in. Its metal walls should contain these things for enough time for you to accomplish what you must."

Lin needed no second command. The things had not yet reached down into Artaxl's feet. He grabbed his feet and dragged him along the floor to the first door.

Edona opened the door. It revealed an empty room with tiers of bunks. Lin dragged Artaxl inside.

"I'll be back," he said. Then he pulled the hatch door shut.

An Indian appeared in the narrow corridor. When he saw them he called anxiously to them in his own language. Edona translated.

"He says there's something wrong with the ship," she said. "Rax wants us in the pilot room at once."

They followed the Indian at a trot as he led the way. Shortly they entered a large room filled with men. There were dead bodies lying unnoticed on the floor—the defenders who had been caught in the ship and slain.

In the center of the group was a white Inca Lin had never seen before. His lips were curled in an expression of contempt.

Rax saw Lin and called to him.

"There was a trap," he said. "The controls were fixed so that when we took off into the four-dimensional trajectory that was supposed to take us into free space, it started an automatically set trajectory that would crash us on Earth I."

Lin's eyes caught sight of a large screen on which was moving a familiar landscape. He had seen San Francisco from the air before, and there was no mistaking its topography.

"Does it matter?" he asked bitterly. "We have the inter-plane drive intended for the planetoid. Even if we get killed we have at least saved the Earth."

"No," Rax said. "This man says Montakotl has another one, and it will be set up on the planetoid in time. We've failed."

"We haven't failed until the worst happens," Lin said. "But we've got to act fast. Are there suits on board to wear in the vacuum of space?"

"Yes," Rax said.

"O.K.," Lin said. "Bring them out. Everybody's got to have one on before we crash."

On the screen San Francisco was gone. The Redwood forest was rushing up at them. Even as Lin watched the forest vanished to be replaced by a view of a different Earth, two miles below them.

There was a flurry of movement about them as spacesuits were brought out of their concealment in lockers. Lin grunted his satisfaction as he saw they were well made, and with parachutes and inter-plane belts built onto them.

He finished getting into the one brought to him in time to see Earth II vanish and be replaced by a small globe a long distance away. That globe was Earth I.

Most of the others were in spacesuits now. Edona stood near him, her eyes bright with confidence as they looked at him.

"Are there no auxiliary controls or means of softening our landing on Earth I?" Lin asked.

"They're all locked," the Inca captive sneered.

"Then we must get into the cargo sphere where the inter-time drive is," Lin said. "There we can be protected by the cushioning springs."

He felt a gloating satisfaction as he saw the look of alarmed anger on the prisoner's face. He had hit on the one method of surviving the fall to Earth I.

Rax led the way. He, and most of the others as well, seemed to know their way about the ship as if they had at some time been on such ships. That was quite likely, since space travel seemed to have been part of the civilization of the Incas for a long time.

In a few minutes they had reached and entered the sphere, walking along narrow catwalks to a much smaller sphere suspended within by spiderwebs of thick coil springs and collapsible tubes.

Not all of them had time to get into the safety of that center sphere before the crash came. There was a thunderous roar and sickening lurch that seemed to shake Lin's head loose from his body within the spacesuit. It was followed by absolute silence.

The silence was so abrupt that Lin suspected he must have blacked out, though he wasn't aware of having lost consciousness.

He tried to stand. There was a swaying, rhythmic motion. The center sphere must still be moving within its frame of coil springs, he concluded.

He thought of Artaxl. Artaxl had undoubtedly been killed by the fall if he were not dead before from the things from the sixth plane. In either case it was a blessed release from his suffering.

Spacesuited figures were stirring now. Some of them were making their way back to the opening through which they had entered this center sphere.

Lin stood up. He was at the base of a huge platform on which rested quite modern looking turbo-generator units and the largest transformer unit he had ever seen. He surmised the transformer unit must be the inter-plane drive with its huge core of heavy-iron.

He recognized Edona's face through the plastic helmet of the spacesuited figure approaching him. He grinned at her and spoke. Her lips moved, but no sound came through. The reason for this struck him. There was no air on Earth I, and in the crash all the air in the ship had escaped.

He stepped toward her and placed his helmet against hers to conduct sound.

"Are you all right, Edona?" he asked anxiously.

"Yes, Lin," she said. "Are you?"

"I think so," he said. "Let's get out of here and see what we've gotten into."

They joined the procession leaving the sphere. In the outer shell they could see the remains of those unfortunates who hadn't had time to reach the center sphere.

The outer sphere had flattened where it had struck. The catwalks were twisted and torn; but they were able to get across to gaping rips in the outer shell and drop to the ground outside.

A scene of indescribable desolation greeted them. Their legs sank to the knees in powdered pumice dust. The landscape was like that which astronomers had said would be found on the moon. There were mountainous craters with jagged ridges.

In the black sky shone the fiery, corona-encircled brilliance of a blindingly white sun. It was small, more like a star of unusual size than a real sun.

"Sun I is small like Earth I is small," Lin concluded.

But now the full meaning of their predicament struck Lin. Here they were, trapped on the surface of an airless planet. Even if the ship had not been damaged in the fall, it had no means of being lifted from the surface. They were trapped just as surely as if they had landed on the moon itself.

Their inter-plane belts would be of absolutely no use here. There was no other body that could pull them out of this first plane. The bulk of Earth II, rising thousands of miles above them, formed a solid hyper-plane that blocked their escape from this plane.

They had survived the fall, but they might have been better off if they had been killed.

He kept these dark thoughts to himself.

Rax found him and showed him and Edona the switch that cut in the two-way radio which would enable them to talk to everyone as easily as if there were air to conduct sound.

Instantly conversational noises flooded Lin's ears. Everyone was on the same wavelength. Lin couldn't understand any of the words he heard. They were all in the two Inca languages.

"What are they saying, Edona?" he asked, making his voice sound carefree.

"They are being very bitter," Edona said, her voice full of pity. "They say they shouldn't have listened to my father, that Montakotl was right. If they hadn't listened they would be in the safety of their homes right now."

"Well," Rax said dryly. "There's nothing they can do about it now. We're trapped, and there's nothing that can rescue us." His voice became bitter. "We've failed completely."

"It looks that way," Lin muttered.

As if to add to their hopelessness there was a sudden screaming noise, borne to them through their radio earphones, and from the wreckage of the spaceship rose three snakelike figures of translucent gray, each as large as a man, moving in the atmosphereless space over the ship by powers unknown.

CHAPTER EIGHT

AS LIN WATCHED, his eyes seemed to adjust more and more to the details of structure of the three things. Though a horror welled up from his very soul, making him want to scream and scream in unleashed, uncontrolled fear, there was a part of his mind that remained apart, calm and clear. It was watching and studying the three things.

They were serpentine, their snake-like bodies arching gracefully, elfin wings near their heads beating swiftly. Yet they were also birdlike, in that instead of the blunt snouts of serpents, they had long sharp beaks and birdlike heads covered with fine feathers that were almost a fuzz.

How could their wings hold them up in an atmosphereless space? In that moment of unnatural clarity of thought Lin understood. These things were not of ordinary matter. Their structure was sub-nuclear, electronic. A living structure such as a human being is an ionic pattern in a medium composed mostly of water. In these creatures the ionic pattern was divorced from the bulky mass of water and dissolved impurities. Almost weightless, their wings probably held them aloft by a sort of inductive action on the space-time composition of the gravity field itself.

While these thoughts were forming with crystal clarity in Lin's mind—or one part of it, rather, in another part something entirely different was going on.

Abstractedly he recognized that the presence of the three cold-plane creatures had induced a state of shock in him. It had split his mind into independent segments. Each problem in his mind had withdrawn itself into its own little sphere under the action of the mind-unbalancing shock.

And in that state he saw clearly what could be done, not only to rescue them from this prison of a planet, but to save Earth III from destruction.

The elfin horns of the three things were sounding in Lin's ears over the radio receiver built into his suit—or were those sounds pure thought alone? There was no way of knowing without shutting off the two-way radio, and there was no time for such idle experimenting.

"Back to the ship," Lin shouted. "Back to the center sphere where we can shut these things out."

The three winged serpents ceased their hovering. Swift as light they darted down, each choosing a separate prey. Their sharp beaks entered three helmets. Three terror stricken voices screamed in agony.

"Back to the ship!" Lin shouted. He took Edona's hand and ran. And as he ran he saw the agonized face of Rax Antl through the plastic helmet of a spacesuit into which one of the things was slowly settling.

Rax would die, and it was his fault. He had not obeyed Artaxl's command to desert him. Artaxl had said to leave him or the world would be destroyed.

The thought gave him added strength. Now that he knew what he must do to save the world, he mustn't let anything stand in his way.

As he reached the entrance to the ship he looked back. Others were coming after him. But still others were falling under the attacks of the three winged serpents as they struck, and rose to strike again.

Together, he and Edona ran along the catwalk to the center sphere, taking giant leaps across broken sections in the weak gravity of Earth I.

They reached the hatch opening to the sphere. Lin stopped and waited as others came across the catwalk. A dozen plunged past him.

But the winged serpents had divined his plan and left their victims to cut off the avenue of escape of the others. They were three streaks of silver-gray as they darted toward the ship.

Lin looked regretfully at the people still struggling toward him. Then his hands, seeming to act of their own volition, shut the hatch cover and twirled the wheel that shot home the bolts.

"Weren't there any more of us?" Edona asked. Lin looked at her and lied.

"That was all," he said. "There were no more. They were all killed by the things."

From the door came angry tappings as the winged serpents tried to break through. Lin smiled grimly. If they were electronic they wouldn't dare to break through. Their structure would be disrupted into eddying electric flows within the conducting bulk of the metal.

But now—there was work to do. Work that perhaps only he could do.

With Edona following him he climbed the ladder welded into the side of the huge base on which the inter-time drive was built. It had been built to kick a small planet from one plane to another.

Had it, too, been tampered with? That didn't seem likely. Montakotl would never think to do that. But until he could get the huge turbo-generators humming he couldn't be sure.

A hasty exploration of the vast floor brought him to a central control section. He breathed a sigh of satisfaction. The controls were standard. The knowledge and know-how that had built this huge unit had been derived from Earth III engineering, at least.

Closer inspection proved that many of the parts, if not all, of the control panels were actually manufactured on Earth III. Standard brand names were stamped on them.

Lin returned to a panel that controlled turbo unit No.1. His fingers, through long experience, manipulated the pistol-grip controls.

There was a whirring vibration rising through the soles of his shoes as a generator somewhere began to operate. The meters came to life. Pointers broke away from their zero pins and crept upward toward red lines that indicated operating values.

He went to another panel and went through the same routine. Then another and another, until all ten turbo units were in operation.

Finally he went to the co-ordinating panel and synchronized one generator after another until they were all connected to the main busses, and the automatic controls that prevented them from draining on each other were working smoothly.

Now there was only one thing left to do.

Lin went to the master panel. Would the thing happen that he hoped for? Or had all his work been in vain?

There was one pistol-grip control relay yet to flick briefly to one side. Without having seen into the maze of wires behind the panel, nor followed those wires to their connections to the generators and busses, he knew what would take place when he flicked that final relay.

There would be a crashing of vacuum disconnects as they came together. Power, more than enough to run a city, would rush through giant copper bars. Automatic controls would run wild. The huge turbines would snarl and whine under sudden overload.

But would the thing happen that he hoped for? There were too many unknowns. An instrument designed for one thing was going to have to do something it was not intended for. If it didn't—

His hand reached out. His fingers touched the innocent looking pistol grip handle sticking out from the panel. There were no meters on this panel. There would be no need for them, nor could they measure the tremendous forces as they surged in unleashed fury once that small relay control was thrown.

He hesitated, his mind full of doubts, his thoughts hastily reviewing everything he had done so far to make sure he had done nothing wrong. The touch of his finger could save or destroy the billions of lives on Earth III, people going their ways oblivious of the fact that their destiny was in the hands of one man in a realm of existence unknown to them: people on subways, people in churches, people at home, relaxed in soft chairs as they read books or watched their television screens that brought them entertainment. Lin hesitated.

And a cold hand gripped his shoulder and spun him about.

Instinctively his hands came up to ward off the blows of the threatening figure. It was a man, but he wore no spacesuit. On his face was a livid scar that went from his jaw across his cheek and through an empty eye socket to his forehead.

Lin's mind froze as he recognized Artaxl. Artaxl was dead, his body crushed from the fall; yet he was here. In his one eye blazed a light of gray fury. Through it watched a mind deranged, controlled by those things from the Sargasso Sea of the sixth plane.

A fist crashed against Lin's helmet. As it struck it bent queerly. A jagged end of white bone shot through the bloodless skin.

Artaxl looked blankly at that jagged bone. The light dimmed in his eyes. In Lin's ears angry flutings sounded rapid and staccato. They ended as abruptly as they had begun.

For an instant it was Artaxl standing there. His lips formed silent words.

"Throw that switch, Lin," they said.

Then Artaxl collapsed, his frame falling slowly to the metal floor as life departed from it.

Lin waited for no more. With a leap he was back to the master panel. His hand shot out and gripped the relay switch control. His wrist twisted.

Darkness descended on him in an engulfing wave, and with it a sound of thunder and rending of metal.

CHAPTER NINE

HE AWAKENED to an absolute silence. Here and there was a feeble light that illuminated the interior of the sphere. Spacesuited figures huddled motionless, nearby, and against the far walls of the sphere.

Lin attempted to rise. He found himself floating upward and not coming down. The implications of this struck him and filled him with happiness. He had succeeded. Weightlessness meant the sphere was either in outer space or in free fall. In either case it could only mean he had won. But where was Edona? Had she survived? Some of the spacesuited figures were in twisted positions that meant their wearers were dead.

"Edona!" he called frantically.

"Here I am, Lin," a voice sounded in his ear. And one of the figures below him waved, then shot up to him as he waved back.

Her momentum carried them both to the top of the sphere, clinging to each other. Lin kicked against the ceiling. They dropped down to the platform on which rested the huge inter-plane drive.

From there Lin shot toward the closed hatch opening to the outer sphere. He opened it and crawled out onto the catwalk. The outer sphere was nearly torn loose from the inner one now. Through jagged rents he could see a canopy of stars.

Suddenly he let out a shout. Through one jagged opening could be seen a huge globe that covered a third of the sky in that direction. It was the Earth!

He called into his two-way radio for the others to come out. One by one they joined Lin and Edona on the catwalk, gripping the handrails, bending over to look below at the sight of the Earth.

It didn't matter which of the four Earths it was; they were far enough away from it so that as they fell they could take their pick.

"It's the Earth," Edona's voice sounded, full of wonder. "But how—?"

Other voices were sounding in the Inca tongues. From their tones they were merely echoing Edona's thoughts.

"Time enough to explain later," Lin said happily. "Right now we'd better get out of here, Edona. Tell them they must all grip hands and hold together while we jump free of this death trap."

Edona spoke in their language. Carefully they carried out Lin's commands. Finally they were all together in space, the sphere growing small as it retreated from them.

"Let go and pull your ripcords," Lin ordered. "When we hit atmosphere your chutes will open and slow your fall."

Here and there the white of the small pilot chute sprang into sight as they obeyed his order.

Hours later Lin threw open the helmet of his spacesuit and breathed in the clean air of Earth V. The others at his order had switched on their inter-plane belts to pull into the Earth-plane with the greatest gravitational attraction.

They drifted down in a compact group under Lin's directions on how to guide their fall by slip-chuting. They landed in a large grassy field.

Now they discarded their spacesuits and gathered about Lin and Edona, asking questions. Lin held up his hands until they were quiet.

"I did the only thing I could do," he said. "Not knowing whether it would work or not. I'll try to explain. I knew that when the huge inter-plane drive was turned on it would cause the entire bulk of Earth I to try to fall into the second Earth-plane, drawn by the attraction of its gravitation field. I knew that Earth II would prevent that. But I hoped that there would be enough force exerted to knock Earth II against Earth III, and so on, so that Earth I would jog all four Earths out of their normal planes. If it did it would bounce them all ahead into a different plane. Then when the approaching planetoid fell it would strike either Earth II or Earth I. In either case Earths III and V would be saved from destruction. If it hit Earth I, being nearly the same size, they would both be knocked into small pieces. If we were lucky enough not to be crushed we would be thrown into space far enough so that when the four Earths swung back again we could return to Earth III or V. That's the way it happened."

"But why would they swing back?" Edona asked.

"Because they would have to," Lin said. "The laws of mechanics would have to hold for the fourth dimension. If Earth I had been completely thrown out into space by the collision they might not be; but enough of the hulk of the planetoid and Earth I would remain to make a large body. And the fourth-dimensional center of mass would still have its original velocity, putting them all back into the planes they had been in. No one alive probably even noticed the momentary change in the position of sun and the moon."

There was rapid talking among the few Inca survivors. Edona listened and informed Lin that they recognized where they were. They were three days' march from their village, lying to the west.

"Sixty miles or less," Lin said. "We could drop down to Earth III right here and catch a bus to Los Angeles and be there in a few hours."

"But my father—" Edona's lips trembled. Tears filmed her eyes as sudden recollection brought grief with it.

"You're right," Lin said contritely.

"I can't leave here until he's received a decent burial," Edona said, as if speaking aloud to herself.

Lin didn't answer. Instead, he took her hand and started walking. The natives took places ahead and behind them, leaving the discarded spacesuits where they lay.

As they trudged along, Lin looked at the ground they walked on and envisioned the California landscape beneath it. Two miles straight down, and perhaps a millionth of an inch at right angles in the fourth space dimension, lay date palms, highways, and the hot desert, with people who could look up into the unobstructed sky and never suspect that they were looking past and through two miles of solid substance lying a small fraction of an inch "outside" the three-dimensional space they believed to contain all reality.

Dimensions were strange things. A straight line makes one dimension. A second one at right angles to it makes two dimensions. A third at right angles to the other two makes a third dimension. Apparently a fourth couldn't be constructed that would be perpendicular to the other three. For that reason common experience gave space as a three dimensional extension. Yet in that space was movement, change of position, so that in giving the location of any object one had to give the time it was there, so that time became a fourth co-ordinate of experience.

And now it developed that besides time there was a fourth space dimension that wasn't time, but actual extension in space the same as the three ordinary dimensions.

Lin considered this strange thing as he walked along beside Edona. Each step carried him between two and three feet along on solid ground—but a slip of a small fraction of an inch in the fourth dimension of space would leave him falling free, two miles above Earth III—or plunge him into the Sargasso Sea of another hyper-slice of space where strange creatures with electronic bodies drifted, hungry.

Such was the narrow line between two unreachable realities. But he himself was just as narrow as the line. He couldn't "fall" to one side without being dragged by something that had four dimensional "reach," like the mysterious heavy-iron.

Perhaps a millionth of an inch away were some of those serpent-like electronic creatures. Or—

What had become of those three that had been with them? Had they survived? Were they now in the space of Earth V hunting for victims to feed on? And what of the others of those things that had come through under the force of Montakotl's weapons? A vague foreboding took possession of Lin. He said nothing about it, but it grew in his mind.

What of the future? Could he be content to take Edona back with him to Los Angeles and forget all about Earth V? How had knowledge of this world—of this setup of worlds within worlds—been kept secret from mankind? Would it remain secret now?

Thus Lin walked along, a scowl of thought on his face, only half seeing the paths he walked along over hills and through grassy meadows and wooded sections. Edona walked beside him, sensing his concentration and not wishing to disturb his thoughts, perhaps half lost in her own.

It was toward evening, the blood red sun half concealed under the western horizon to the south of the high mountain that was their goal, that they came to the broad swath of splintered trees and trampled grass.

Lin was jerked out of his reverie by the excited murmurs of the natives' voices as they halted. They were clustered together talking, and pointing to the ground. When he reached them he looked down where they pointed.

There were tracks such as might have been made by many elephants running. Out of the native speech one word settled in Lin's mind. It was a word being repeated many times. It had a very familiar sound to it, as though he had heard it before someplace. That word was "Xinli." It was evidently what they called the animals that had made the tracks and layed flat so much ground.

"They say the Xinli must have been pursued by something awful to stampede like this," Edona translated for Lin's benefit. "I don't know what the Xinli are. I've never seen one, though I've heard them mentioned before. They're some enormous wild animal that's so big it can't be killed easily."

She listened some more.

"They say the Xinli must have passed this way some time ago or the ground would still be shaking," she translated. "If we had been standing within a mile of here when they passed this way in such a stampede, we couldn't have kept on our feet from the vibration of their pounding on the ground."

There was more discussion. Finally the natives took up their journey once again, but not without continual, half fearful watching.

Lin studied the damage done by the stampede as it had rushed through wooded tracts and over grassy ground. He decided some of the creatures must be much heavier than an ordinary elephant.

It took half an hour to cross the swath. When they came to the far edge of it they were where the earth was soft. The huge footprints were at least five inches deep where they had pressed the sod into the ground.

A set of footprints led off at a sharp angle from the main swath. Lin studied it and made a surprising discovery. One foot of the creature had a distinctive marking. It was a left foot. And that was the only type of footprint on the left side. That meant the creature had been running on two feet!

Something clicked in Lin's mind. He remembered suddenly where he had seen the word, Xinli, before. It had been in a story, a work of supposed fiction, written by a man named Merritt.

The major features of that old story came back to him, and with that memory he felt the hair on the nape of his neck rise.

Other things began to click in his mind. The age of reptiles with its dinosaurs, pterodactyls, and other giant creatures had ended abruptly and mysteriously with the advent of warm blooded creatures. Had it been because they had stumbled onto the hidden doorways between this world and Earth III?

What of the winged serpents? Were they the Watchers of that story Merritt had written?"

What of the mystery of Mt. Shasta? Were it, and other high mountains, gateways into Earth V? What of ancient legends that placed the gods at the top of Mount Olympus?

What of Charles Forte's gathered evidence of the falling of mysterious objects from the sky? What of Shaver's so-called caves beneath the Earth in which distorted humans were supposed to live and delight in torturing people?

What of all the thousands of mysteries, disappearances, materializations of strange beings, teleportation of objects through solid walls?

What of Christianity's Hell down below and Heaven up in the sky?

As Lin followed the natives, Edona guiding him along, a new, tremendously broad vista of mystery settled into a vague panorama in his mind. A panorama that encompassed so much and implied so much that his head spun at its vastness.

His scientific experience was already detailing experiments he wanted to try. Some of them would be along the lines Dr. Morell had followed, including the so-called instrument of cold, which was merely a variation of the inter-plane belt, in all probability.

But there were other experiments he wanted to work on. He would have to find a place where Earth III and Earth V had surfaces in common to build a makeshift laboratory. There things could be done without having to fall a couple of miles or climb a couple of miles into the atmosphere of Earth III.

Eventually he could gather other scientists around him and really accomplish things. Surgeons could perform four dimensional surgery without cutting into people. Physicists could experiment with four dimensional fields…

The natives halted and started making camp for the night. Lin snapped out of his dreams and helped. The evening meal consisted of boiled, tuberous roots that tasted somewhat like turnips, a bitter tea, and berries that looked like black gooseberries and had a taste similar to the ordinary variety.

It was while they were eating around the campfire that they felt the slight tremor that told of stampeding tons of mountainous flesh, far away. The Xinli were returning—or were they? The shaking in the ground died down finally.

Bedding consisted of branches from the trees with long, grass-like leaves. Edona and Lin lay down on their beds, close enough so that they could reach across and hold each other's hand—and that was the way Edona finally slept, her fingers slipping from Lin's slowly.

It was long after before he slept. He lay wide awake, his thoughts churning with plans for the future. Once, just before he dozed off, the ground began to shake again from the approach of the giant Xinli—but there were guards that would stay awake part of the night, to be relieved by others, who would warn them if any danger came...

CHAPTER TEN

LIN AWOKE with the pleasant smell of the wood fire in his nostrils, blended with the slightly tangy odor of his bed of branches and the damp grassy smell of earth.

The sun, not yet above the horizon, was just beginning to dispel the shadows of night. The tops of the trees were swaying in a breeze that didn't reach down to the ground.

He lay there, uncomprehending, luxuring in the pleasantness of mere existence, while his mind gradually awakened to the memory of where he was and why.

Then he turned his head to look at Edona. She was still asleep, her face relaxed and innocent. Beautiful. She lay on her back, her breast rising and falling slowly in the rhythm of sleep, her legs pulled up sideways so that her hip was raised in graceful arch. One arm crossed her waist. The other lay, palm upward, as though reaching for his own. It was possible she hadn't moved all night.

Lin's eyes were diverted from Edona by a rapid motion near the smoldering fire. It was one of the Indians, motioning for him to rise and come over.

When he stood up and went over to the man, he turned and walked into the trees. Lin followed. They went several hundred yards, emerging on a scene that brought a gasp of astonishment to Lin's lips.

The trees in an area a hundred feet across had been trampled and broken like matchsticks. Lying half in this trampled area and half concealed in unbroken forest was the limp mass of a giant lizard creature, its rough granite hide glistening with morning dew.

Others of the Indians were walking around, talking to one another in low voices. Lin's guide joined these and pointed out to Lin what was interesting them so much.

Here and there on the creature's hide the dew was, not dew, but white frost. Frost that was perceptibly thick, as though the flesh were frozen and had been frozen for several hours.

Lin didn't need an interpreter to know what the Indians were saying. This could be only the work of the cold creatures from the Sargasso Sea of the sixth plane! And that meant that his foreboding of the evening before was true. The weapons of cold had brought into the realm of Earth V a scourge that could not be fought.

Lin's heart sank. Maybe some of the winged serpents were still in the Xinli carcass. They might come out at any moment and attack them.

"So this is the reason for the stampeding of the Xinli," he said aloud. His guide nodded grimly, having sensed the meaning of Lin's remark.

Horror grew in Lin's thoughts. A mental picture arose of hundreds of these giant creatures racing madly, with the wispy bodies of the winged serpents over them, darting down to settle on their prey. Other thousands of the serpents mantling the city of the Incas, dealing freezing death to its inhabitants.

Was there no way to destroy the winged serpents—the Watchers? But they were not watchers! They were hostile to the Incas. Were there some that were friendly and some that were hostile?

Lin wished he could know. But he was afraid, desperately afraid, that he would never be able to learn. Almost certainly they would be attacked before they reached the village and the safety of the cavern headquarters—if it were a place of safety.

He had to reach it. He had to get there and see if he could devise some protection against the winged serpents of death.

But if they were to stay here, so near this giant thing that might be harboring some of the things—

Lin turned abruptly and raced back the way he had come. In his thoughts anxiety for the safety of Edona forced everything else out. But she was still lying where he had left her, and still asleep.

The Indians had followed him more slowly, leaving one of their number behind. Lin was to learn later that he had been selected by lot to remain there and invite the winged serpents into his body if they emerged from the Xinli, so that the others would have a chance to escape.

Edona awoke as Lin reached the fire. She sat up and smiled sleepily at him, then became aware of the expression on his face and the undertone of fear about her.

She spoke demandingly to the Indians in their tongue. They answered reluctantly. Her eyes widened as she listened to their words.

"What father said was true then," she said to Lin. "We must get to the village and get his instrument. He showed me how it could be used to protect us by reversing the field so that the cold would be forced to enter it and return to the sixth plane again."

"Then he had solved that problem," Lin said, relieved. "Let's get going."

There was a hasty breakfast of what was left of their dinner of the night before. While they were eating there came the sound of a scream. The Indians paled perceptibly, then made hasty signs that they should all start out.

Edona frowned at their words as they talked with one another, as they half trotted away from the campfire into the woods.

"They say that scream was a signal that the living cold has emerged from the Xinli," she said to Lin. "I wonder what they mean."

"One of them stayed near the Xinli," Lin exclaimed. "The winged serpents must have settled into him. They won't waste much time on him. They'll know we're near, and try to find us. Stay close to me, Edona. We still have our chutes, and if they find us we can drop into Earth III."

Edona hugged his side as they trotted through the trees. Lin took her hand. There was a choked feeling in his throat as he thought of the bravery of the Indian who had stayed there to sacrifice his life so the others could be warned in time to escape if escape were possible.

Two of the Indians were running close beside them, the others strung out ahead and behind. Suddenly Lin felt himself thrown to the ground. He threw out his hands to break his fall, and turned his head when he came to a stop. One of the Indians had thrown him. The other had thrown Edona.

The reason was quickly apparent. Above the tree tops appeared one of the winged serpents, its body a shimmer of glowing, transparent milkiness, its wings two gossamer arcs of blurred motion. It paused there, its pointed beak extended downward, then dropped.

One of the Indians was standing, arms outstretched, to receive it, a mixture of horror and resignation on his face. As Lin watched, the pointed beak dipped into the Indian, and slowed. The man screamed in agony, dropping to the ground, unconscious.

Slowly the shadowy serpent form settled into his body until it was out of sight.

"Un!" the Indian holding Lin grunted. He rose, lifting Lin. The other was lifting Edona. In a moment they were again speeding through the trees.

The horror of it all was seeping into Lin's soul. And the nobility of it. The sacrifice of those two Indians who had chosen to die so that others might live.

The others, obviously, were he and Edona. The Indians would sacrifice themselves one by one to save them.

It was awful to think of men dying deliberately to save him. As he ran doggedly along, Lin tried to think of some other way out of this. They were still two days march from the cavern.

He and Edona wore the inter-plane belts. They could escape to Earth III. The Indians couldn't. They would have to keep on toward the village and its doubtful protection. They might be picked off one by one anyway, almost certainly so.

Lin bit his lips. It was horrible to think it, but the Indians themselves recognized that they were expendable and he wasn't. There was a remote chance of his finding some way to destroy the winged death or send it back from whence it had come. As long as that chance existed he must keep on, get through to the village.

But wouldn't it be better to get there as quickly as possible? And might not the Indians, freed of the responsibility of keeping him alive, have that much more chance of escaping the serpents?

Lin watched them covertly as he ran beside Edona. They were obviously able to run much faster than they were going, but were pacing themselves to keep him and Edona from tiring too much.

"Edona," Lin said without slowing his pace, "if we dropped down to our own Earth and went to Los Angeles by bus we could save a whole day, and the Indians wouldn't have to go so slow. They could get there at least half a day sooner without us."

Edona's face brightened. She spoke in the language of the Indians. The Indian beside her grunted his approval.

"All right, Lin," she said.

"I'll count to three," Lin said thinly, dreading the change that would switch them out of this world. "One, two, three!"

He pressed the button on his belt that would do it. As the trees and the ground faded and he felt himself falling he wondered if there might not be a hill or mountain right here so that there wouldn't be time for their chutes to open and break their fall. But it was too late to return now.

Lin recognized the San Bernadino Mountains just to the west. He had flown over this country enough so that in a few moments he knew just where he was. A mile below and slightly to the north was Riverside, California. He smiled in satisfaction.

"Yoo hoo!" Edona, below and behind him, waved cheerily as he twisted his head in the direction of the sound. He waved back, and impulsively slip-chuted toward her until she motioned him away and he realized he was endangering them both.

He looked down at the familiar scenery again, feeling a warm glow of happiness seep through him. Here they were safe. Here they could catch a bus, and if the slightest danger appeared it would be dealt with by the Government and its two hundred million citizens, not a handful of semi-civilized members of a lost race of people in a wild country.

Maybe Edona, now that she was here, would consent to leave her father's body where it was, and stay here.

As quickly as the thought formed, Lin was ashamed of it. Following that course would merely stall things. There were the gateways from Earth V to Earth III. Through those gateways the winged serpents would eventually come when they had sated their hunger on the life of Earth V and there was nothing left alive for them to feed on. They would be a ravening horde, catching the world unprepared.

He looked down again at the warm familiarity of the streets of Riverside, drifting up toward him, and realized that its welcome was temporary—that he could never again call Earth III his home until he had driven the hordes of outer space back into their prison plane.

Yes, and made Montakotl pay for his rashness in bringing them into the fifth plane with his weapons of cold. He had been a stupid child, playing with toys he couldn't fully understand.

The real fault lay with those ancients who had not destroyed those weapons, but left them around for posterity to play with.

Still, how could those ancients have foreseen the future? The very same thing could happen with modern weapons. The vast stockpiles of atom bombs, assembled and ready to use, could become the same kind of a thing. A devastating war could destroy civilization, leaving nothing but distorted legend in its place; and ignorant savages, descendants of the survivors of such a war, could one day bring out atom bombs to use in some petty quarrel with a neighboring tribe—and destroy them all including themselves.

Undoubtedly those ancients who had used the weapons of cold had known how to control the winged serpents and force them to go back into the sixth plane. Otherwise they wouldn't have built and used such things.

And it would be up to him to rediscover their secrets.

As Lin's feet struck the ground he realized that he had to find the answer. He and Edona would get to Los Angeles as quickly as possible and return to Earth V the way he had entered it the first time.

Edona landed fifty feet away, seconds later. Lin had gathered his chute into a bundle under his arm.

"I'm all right, Lin," she said when he rushed to her, an anxious look on his face.

Together they folded both chutes carefully and put them back in their packs. While they were doing it, several cars collected on the highway a short distance away, and men were starting across the field toward them.

"Hallo!" one of them called. "Are you all right?"

"Yes, we're all right," Lin said, smiling at the men as they came up. "But we have to get to Los Angeles as soon as possible. Any of you going that way?"

"I am," one of them said, stepping forward. "That's where I was headed when I saw you two up in the sky. What happened to your plane?"

"It was having trouble," Lin lied. "Our pilot ordered us out. He's trying to make it to Los Angeles."

"Hope he makes it," the man said. "My name's Gates. Arthur Gates. If you're in a hurry, come on. I'll get you there fast."

"Thanks," Lin said. "Come on, Edona." He took her arm.

Two minutes later they were on their way to Los Angeles, the car they were in eating up the miles smoothly.

"I didn't get your names," Arthur Gates said, glancing at Lin questioningly.

"Sorry," Lin said. "I'm Lin Carter, and this is Edona Morell."

"Lin Carter," Gates said slowly, flavoring the name. "Sounds familiar. Say! That's the name of the fellow that disappeared from the cockpit of a plane a few days ago." His eyes turned to Edona. "Had a girl with him, too. You the ones?"

"Disappeared from the cockpit of a plane?" Lin asked, stalling. He wished now he hadn't given his right name. It would have been simpler not to.

"Yeah," Arthur Gates said. "Funniest thing. The pilot swore it was impossible, but both of you just vanished. No way you could, but you weren't there. You never landed anywhere, either."

"Must have been someone else," Lin said with a short laugh.

"Lot of funny things lately," Gates said, ducking around a car skillfully in the traffic. "I suppose you know about the Sun behaving funny yesterday. I saw it myself. Lasted just a second or two."

"Uh huh," Lin said vaguely.

"You see it?" Gates asked.

"Uh-no," Lin said. "I was asleep at the time. What'd it look like to an eyewitness?"

"One minute the sun was itself," Gates said, "the next instant it was twice as big and a cherry red instead of white. Then it was back again the way it was, but sort of in and out, for almost half an hour. Reports from Asia say a huge moon ten times as big as real life appeared suddenly in the sky, then vanished again. Several people in India swore that they were looking at the moon about that time, and it was suddenly only half as big as normal, and its crescent was red instead of white. Very mysterious business. And not only that. Right this minute there's a tidal wave in the Pacific that's coming toward America.

It'll be here in a couple of days, and will raise the tide to the highest point in history. They're evacuating the coastline right now."

"Yes, I know all that," Lin smirked. "I was just wondering how the sun looked to an eyewitness. Did it *grow* bigger and smaller, or just change suddenly?" He looked innocently at Arthur Gates.

"It changed suddenly," Gates replied, relaxing visibly.

"Interesting," Lin murmured.

The conversation lagged. Lin and Edona watched the scenery slide by. The sky was very blue. Except for an occasional white billow of cloud it was empty.

There was nothing to indicate that less than a millionth of an inch from every atom in their body was an atom of solid stone, two miles below the surface of Earth V.

Two objects cannot occupy the same space, but two objects can have the same three-space co-ordinates so long as they are separated in the fourth dimension. They are two extremely thin hyper-planes lying against each other loosely, hardly affecting one another, the basic nature of reality in some way ordering them separately.

"Where do you want to go?" Arthur Gates asked, breaking into Lin's thoughts.

Lin blinked his eyes and noted they were coming into Southgate.

"We're going to the airport at Gardena," he said. "If that's out of your way, you can let us out at a taxi stand."

"Be glad to take you over," Gates said, smiling. "That where your plane's going to land?"

"Possibly," Lin said. "Anywhere it can get to that there's an airport, more likely."

Gates turned off onto an east-west arterial. Fifteen minutes later he was turning into the Gardena airport. He pulled into a parking space and shut off the car.

"You stopping here too?" Edona asked in surprise.

"Why not?" Gates grinned. "This is interesting."

"Thanks for the ride," Lin said. "How much do we owe you?"

"Not a cent," Gates grinned. "I'm a reporter. I'll make mine on the story."

"Oh," Lin said. He was climbing out of the car as he spoke. Edona followed him. Lin slammed the car door at the same time as Gates on the other side.

The three of them went into the airport office. There were several people there, one of them the pilot who had taken them up before. He recognized them, his eyes widening in surprise.

"Mr. Carter!" he said.

"So you weren't the ones," Gates snorted. Then, to the pilot, "Believe it or not, Wilson, they just landed over by Riverside."

Others were converging on them excitedly.

"How did it happen?" Wilson, the pilot, asked. "Am I glad you showed up. Everybody was beginning to think I was crazy."

"We haven't time to explain," Lin said. "We've got to go up again right away. Can you take us?"

"Sure," Wilson said doubtfully, "but—"

"How about telling us what it's all about, Carter," Gates said. "And don't tell me you don't know. You vanished from Wilson's plane deliberately. What gives?"

He followed his question with an appealing, but determined smile. Lin frowned, then matched the smile.

"I'll tell you," he said mysteriously, "but don't breathe a word of it in your paper. We travelled into the fourth dimension to another world two miles above this one, where we met the descendants of the Incas. We were trying to get away from some giant dinosaurs that were being stampeded by some snakes made out of electricity instead of matter, when the flying serpents started attacking us, so we came back, using our parachutes to land with, since when we stepped into the fourth dimension we were two miles up in the air. We have to go back right away because Edona forgot her lipstick."

"Verra phonya," Arthur Gates said dryly. "I don't believe any of it except about the lipstick," he added, looking at Edona's unadorned lips. Then, to Wilson, "You gonna take them up again?"

"I guess so," Wilson answered. "He paid for the first trip. Want to go along so I'll have a witness if they vanish again?"

CHAPTER ELEVEN

"LET ME GET this straight," Gates said. "When you press a button on that queer looking belt you and Edona have around your waists you're pulled in a direction at right angles to all directions we have in space, and enter another space lying next to this one. I don't believe it."

"I don't care whether you do or not," Lin said. "In a couple of minutes now you'll see it happen."

Arthur Gates studied Lin in exasperated silence. He looked out at the California landscape far below. His eyes squinted upward as though trying to "see" if there were something there he couldn't see normally.

"Look," he said finally, "if what you say is true I want to come along."

"But you can't," Edona said. "We only have the two belts."

But even as she said it her eyes lit up at a sudden recollection.

"There may be another," she added. "I think father made some extras and left them at our place in the mountains."

"Well, let's go see," Arthur Gates said. "I think you could use another hand where you're going."

Lin hesitated, but finally decided Gates was right. And so, several hours later, they were again where they had been, but this time Arthur Gates also wore a parachute pack and a belt. He was a little pale. When Edona pressed on her belt and melted through the seat with her pilot chute unfurling, Lin was sure Gates would back down, but he didn't.

"You next," Lin said, a twisted smile on his lips.

Gates hesitated visibly, then jabbed the right button and followed Edona, while the pilot, Wilson, forgot to breathe. This time he was seeing the actual disappearance.

Lin followed the instant he was sure Gates would he clear. He closed his eyes as he pressed the pin on the belt, counted to ten, pulled the ripcord, and opened his eyes.

He should have pulled the ripcord sooner. When he opened his eyes he was below the other two parachutes, and the clearing was only two or three hundred feet above him. He watched trees rush up at him and wondered if he would slow down enough to light without breaking some bones. The chute caught the air and slowed him down rapidly. He landed without injury, but with a feeling that if he'd counted to eleven he would have been killed.

Moments later Edona and Arthur Gates dropped near him. They laughed and talked nervously as they folded up the chutes and put them back in their packs for instant use.

"I believe it now," Arthur said earnestly. He looked down at the grassy solidity under his feet. "To think that a couple of miles down there is California…"

"And don't ever forget it," Lin said. "At any time we might be attacked by the winged serpents. If you see one coming toward you, press the button that plunges you over, and you'll be safely out of this world."

All three looked nervously about. The trees were motionless in the still air. The meadow in the clearing was serene. The sky was devoid of all motion other than a few drifting clouds.

"Let's go," Edona said nervously.

They found the path into the forest and followed it in its windings toward the distant mountain to the west.

"That mountain is over the ocean, isn't it?" Arthur Gates asked. "Then if we change over when we get there, we'll land in the ocean."

"That will be better than the freezing death," Lin said. "We've seen it, and know. In the ocean you might be picked up. The worst that could happen would be to drown."

"Is that better?" Gates asked dubiously.

Half an hour later he decided it would be. A quotl lay beside the path, its moose-like form still moving feebly, frost congealing on its fur. They had come on it suddenly, stood looking at it in stunned surprise.

"Let's get out of here," Lin said urgently. "The winged serpent might come out of it any second and see us."

Gates needed no urging. His dazed senses were bringing him a literal barrage of facts to switch his beliefs around to the point where he realized that the lipstick was the only fiction in the glib story Lin had told at the airport.

Evening came as they reached the foothills and the swift stream. With it came a cool breeze, and with the breeze came chilling sounds of flutings from far away.

The eerie sounds came from the direction of the Inca city, Montaca. Lin heard them and pictured hordes of the transparent creatures swarming over the city, dipping down to kill and kill and kill. Would there be anyone left alive?

There was an unearthly beauty of tone in the short, fluid piping's that drifted to the ear over such great distance. They were similar to the tinkle of glass against glass, but almost with the quality of speech.

Edona stayed close to Lin. Arthur Gates was subdued and silent, concentrating on walking. At times Lin was grateful for the protection of the trees that hid their progress. At other times he wondered if it were less a protection than a cloak to hide the approach of winged serpents if they came this way.

At last they reached the base of the cliffs that reared upward to unseeable heights in gloom shrouded silence. They picked their way carefully along the base of the cliff while the white spray of the torrent in the river channel licked at their feet hungrily.

They went in single file, gripping hands so that if one slipped the others could prevent a dangerous fall. When they came to the place where they had to step from stone to stone they welcomed the white foam of the water that outlined each place to step.

Lin thought of the sentinel far up on the face of the cliff and wondered if he had seen their coming and notified the others left here. He thought of Dr. Morell's body lying on a cot inside the mountain. He thought finally of Mara. Would she grieve at the news of Rax's death? Or was she still here? Might she have gone to Montaca to her half brother, Montakotl?

The cliffs moved back from their path. The white veil of the waterfall came into view, and, to one side, the sharp cornered dark forms of the buildings of the village.

But Lin hardly noticed these familiar things, and from Arthur Gates startled grunt he hadn't noticed them at all. In the space above the buildings between the cliffs, with the waterfall as a backdrop, a battle was being fought.

It was alien, yet as familiar as the flying struggle of fighting sparrows in general pattern. The fighters were all winged serpents, seemingly two factions pitted against each other.

Lin pulled Edona and Arthur Gates back into the concealment of the cliff.

"Quiet," he warned in a whisper. "If they see us we're gonners."

He peeked around the concealment of out jutting rock and studied the fighting creatures in the air. Two of them, their snake-like bodies writhing in eel-like motion while their almost insectine wings beat in blurred motion, darted from the group, paused in midair, their long sharp beaks turning this way and that as if sniffing, then shot directly toward Lin.

Even as they did so, four others disengaged themselves from the battle and shot to catch them. The six met in battle scant yards away, their bodies weaving in serpentine thrusts of incredible grace and rhythm.

Lin, forgetting his danger or perhaps sensing the futility of trying to escape, stood in plain sight of the battling serpents, watching in admiration and awe.

Suddenly a transparent beak found a mark in the body of another. The beak tilted downward, the victim of the thrust sliding off, to flutter down to the surface of the boiling stream. Even before it hit the water its form seemed to be melting and evaporating.

There were no distinguishing marks for Lin to tell whether the fatality had been one of the two who had apparently spotted him, or one of the four. Nor did it seem to make any difference.

But now it became apparent it had been one of the two, for the other four concentrated on the remaining one of the pair. In seconds the battle over Lin's head was over, with a second transparent form dropping and evaporating into nothingness.

The four victors hovered motionless, with blurred wings beating, for the space of a long breath. Then a beak turned to point directly at Lin. The owner of the beak dropped swiftly down toward him.

His hand went to his belt to press the button that would send him into the plane of Earth III. It hesitated. A voice that was no more than a thought forced itself into his mind.

"Wait!" it said. "Remain where you are and don't move, and you will be safe."

With blurred motion the four winged serpents shot up and into the main battle again, while Lin watched their departure with amazement.

Were there friendly members of this sixth-plane race of things? Was that the cause of the fighting?

Lin leaned against the cliff, weak from the imminence of death in such a horrible form. His mind was spinning, struggling with indecision. He felt Edona's hand on his arm.

"They were friendly," she whispered in his ear. That bears out what Artaxl told me once about them—that long ago his ancestors had made an eternal pact with some of them that could never be broken."

"They must be fighting for the villagers," Lin said softly. "If they win out we can make it to the cavern in the cliff. If not, we'll have to parachute down to Earth III. All we can do is wait."

They huddled together, gaining strength from mutual contact, watching the aerial battle. More and more of the winged creatures were dropping, pierced by the sharp beaks of others.

Finally a small part of the swirling fighters separated from the rest and rose swiftly, passing overhead as they fled between the cliff walls.

The swirling mass of the remaining winged serpents slowed to quiescence. Then, while the three watched, they slowly vanished where they hovered. But they were not gone. An occasional flute-like note came from overhead to indicate they were still there, though invisible.

Hesitantly, his finger resting lightly on the button that would take him out of the plane of Earth V, Lin stepped away from the protection of the cliff into the open. He took several steps, slowly. Nothing happened.

He motioned with his hand for Edona and Arthur Gates to follow him. He led the way to the cliff house where the entrance to the tunnel was hidden.

Once he thought he felt the wind of beating wings against his cheek. A warm thought of safety crept into his mind, reassuringly. But he couldn't be sure it wasn't imagination. He was still dazed at the possibility of some of these creatures being allies rather than destroyers. He still wasn't sure.

If there were any human survivors in the village they were hidden. Lin led the way up the ladder to the level of the room concealing the tunnel entrance. Once again he was staring at the unbroken face of the cliff inside the bare room while Edona reached under a rough projection near the floor and did things which caused a section of the wall to move back.

Once again there was revealed a tunnel which Lin knew led deep into the mountain. As they entered it there came, faintly, the thin piping's of the invisible winged serpents.

To Lin it was a sound of new hope. It meant that the menace of the winged serpents was being met—by other winged serpents. It meant much more; but as the huge bulwark of stone rose behind them in the tunnel, he was suddenly very tired. A load had been lifted from his shoulders, leaving him weak.

Thus he was caught completely by surprise by what lay waiting for his return in the main cavern.

CHAPTER TWELVE

THE EMPTINESS that the scene outside had created within Lin and Edona made it inevitable that when they emerged from the tunnel into the main cavern and saw the dozens of people they would compensate by rushing forward, throwing caution to the winds. And Arthur Gates, following their lead in this strange land he knew nothing about, would not be suspicious unless they were.

Edona was the first to suspect something wrong and try to retreat. It was too late. Too late even to escape to the third plane of Earth.

Lin managed to get in one ineffectual blow against a red shoulder before he was borne to the stone floor by sheer weight of attacking numbers. His arms were firmly held by half a dozen strong hands when he was pulled to his feet, to find Edona and Gates also held the same way.

The Indians crowding around them curiously drew apart as two figures pushed their way through. One of them was a man, white skinned, tall, with a haughty lift to his chin that seemed habitual. Around his neck twined a narrow band of gold in the shape of a serpent, with two small eyes of red emerald. Those small red eyes, rather than the face of the man, held Lin's attention hypnotically—until he became aware that the second person was Mara.

Together with recognition of her came the realization that this man must be her half brother, Montakotl. He turned his eyes to the man with new interest.

Montakotl was as tall as he himself, a little over six feet, a skin white and flawless as a woman's, lips over which hovered a mixture of amusement and cruelty, with not a trace of friendliness. His hair, a lustrous black, was combed straight back from his high forehead in smooth waves, to fall in back and form a background of jet for the white of his bare neck above the golden serpent.

Lin's eyes shifted to Mara again. She was looking at him in a dreamy, gloating way. As his eyes contacted hers and held, he felt a tight constriction in his chest. It was as though, by looking into her eyes, she had undressed, to stand before him unclothed, inviting. A dull flush warmed his face. He became aware of the curve of her breasts under her clinging robe of bright crimson with its adornments of jewels. Her red lips curled in a mixture of invitation, promise, and amusement.

Then, suddenly, she noticed Arthur Gates. Her eyes switched to him. She looked at him speculatively. The spell was broken. He turned his head to Edona. Anger flooded his mind at the sight of rough hands holding her arms. But his own were now tied together at his back and he was held by several heavy hands so he could do nothing.

Montakotl spoke briefly. Mara answered without looking at him. Montakotl fixed his eyes on Lin, coldly. They flicked to Edona as he said something, then back again.

"He blames you for the invasion from the sixth plane, Lin," Edona said. "I'm afraid he intends to take it out on us."

"You are quite right," Mara said. "We have plans for you two."

Edona made no answer to that, but her eyes filled with pity for Mara.

"Mara," Lin said gently, "Rax is dead. He was killed by the flying serpents brought from the sixth plane by your half brother's soldiers with their weapons of cold."

He watched her, hoping for some sign of grief. Instead, a look of contempt flashed over her features.

"He was a fool, he and Artaxl," she spat.

Lin's shoulders drooped hopelessly. These people, Mara, Montakotl, and the others, were savages. Little mercy or clear thinking could be expected from them. And now Montakotl gave a brittle order that destroyed all hope.

In response to Montakotl's words the Indians roughly stripped off the belt and parachute that each of the three wore. Without them they were doomed to remain on Earth V.

Montakotl barked another order. Lin's captors dragged him forward past the fire in the center of the cavern toward one of the dark openings leading to side rooms. He turned his head and saw Edona and Arthur Gates being similarly led off.

The last thing he saw before being shoved into a bare stone room was Mara's eyes following him, gloating. A heavy door closed behind him, and he was alone.

For several minutes the room was in darkness except for a narrow crack above and below the door where light from the main cavern came in. Gradually, as his eyes adjusted, the details of his prison became perceptible.

He stood in the center of the room, torn between the desire to get some much needed sleep and the desire to explore the possibilities of escape. The room appeared to be cut into solid rock with no other exit than the heavy door; but he knew from the cunning way the tunnel from the village was concealed by a stone block that it was entirely possible there was a way of escape through some concealed opening.

The thought occurred to him that if it was there Mara would have known about it and he would not have been put here, but in another chamber where there was no secret way of escape. With that, he decided the best thing to do would be to sleep and gain strength for whatever might come.

There was a mat of dried grass against the wall that had evidently seen plenty of use, it was so packed down. He took off his shoes and lay down, cupping his head in his hands, his eyes open.

His thoughts turned to the winged serpents from the sixth plane. From the sounds of their flutings from the direction of Montaca, and from the number of those that had been engaged in aerial fighting outside over the village, there seemed too many of them to have come through via the weapons of cold. Had they been scooped out of their plane by the jolting Earth V had taken, which plunged it into that plane for a moment? That seemed an obvious conclusion.

Lin frowned in thought, trying to recall what he had read in Merritt's works of so-called fiction about the creatures. How much had Merritt known or suspected or had he known anything? Might he not have written what he thought to be pure fiction, but which was actual truth, *gained by unconscious psychic powers,* either by accident or by someone's deliberate design?

In Merritt's "The Face in the Abyss" the winged serpents had been described too exactly for mere imaginative coincidence. And they had been obedient to the wishes of a creature Merritt had called the "Snake Mother." Merritt had even mentioned weapons similar to the weapon of cold. It all tied in. Even Merritt's use of the term, Xinli, for naming the giant prehistoric creatures.

And hundreds of items in Charles Forte's books pointed to the line separating Earth V from Earth III being thin enough so that now and then things did pass over from Earth V and fall to the surface of the only world modern man knew to exist around him. Perhaps many of the mysterious disappearances of people and things were the result of a similar jumping over from the world to Earth II, whose surface was a couple of miles beneath the surface of Earth III.

In addition to those two, there was Richard Shaver and his "Shaver Mystery" of the late nineteen forties, in which he claimed to have proof that there were people living two miles below the earth's surface in caves, with all sorts of weapons, including rays that could affect the human mind. Shaver had claimed there were entrances to the caves from the surface.

He had also claimed that voices that medically insane people "hear" in their heads, and most people sometimes hear, due to freakish pranks of their mind, were in reality induced by instruments used by people in that underground world.

Lin, lying on his back and staring at the stone ceiling of the chamber, recalled a report on an experiment performed by brain surgeons. They had opened the cranium of a living person and touched the brain with a fine wire carrying a mild electric current. Instead of a sensation of being shocked, the person's conscious mind was flooded with thoughts and memories that had nothing to do with what had been going on there just before. Many repetitions of the experiment had established beyond doubt that irritation of the brain produced these effects.

Those surgeons had had to cut open the skull to make the brain accessible. From the second or the fifth plane it would be possible to have some small device such as a fine wire carrying a small current, and by means of the principle used to go from one plane to another the end of the wire could be moved into the same spot as the brain of a person, and transported that millionth of an inch separating the two hyper-planes in the fourth dimension, and you would have the same result.

Lin made a mental resolution to find out more about Earth II if he ever got out of Earth V again.

He awoke with a start and realized he had fallen asleep. He sat up, wondering what had awakened him. There was no way of telling how long he had been asleep.

There was a sound at the door. It was a faint scratching, as though someone wanted to attract his attention without making any noise that could be heard any distance.

He went over to the door and placed his ear against its thick panel. The scratching sound came again, definitely on the door.

"Yes?" Lin said inquiringly.

"This is Mara, Lin," a soft voice sounded. It came from the crack under the door. Lin got down on his knees and held his ear as close to the crack as he could get. "Can you hear me, Lin?" Mara asked.

"Yes," Lin whispered. "What do you want?" His heart was racing loudly.

"I want to come in," Mara said, "but you must promise not to try to escape, and to let me out again. I want to talk with you."

"All right," Lin said quickly. "I promise."

There was a cautious scraping sound halfway up the door. It cracked open, a line of light rising its full length. Then it swung open. Mara's lithe figure was outlined in the light as she darted in and closed the door behind her. She stood against it, her head turning this way and that, searching. Lin realized she couldn't see him yet.

"Where are you?" she asked anxiously.

"Here," he said. He reached out and touched her on the shoulder. Her hand came up and seized his wrist, followed it to his shoulder.

Immediately she was against him, her arms around his neck, her vibrant body pressed against his. Dazedly he tried to avoid her hungrily seeking lips, to draw away. Then she kissed him with unleashed passion, her breath hot and swift against his face.

He fought against her with all his mind while his body remained limp, but her passion was too much to resist. His arms went around her slim waist, hesitant from inner conflict. His lips stopped avoiding hers, then searched for hers as hungrily as her own.

For a long, ecstatic eternity his senses reeled, then her lips went slack, unresisting, her arms slid away from their fierce embrace, her warm body went limp in his arms. She would have fallen if he had not caught her.

He picked her up and carried her to the mat of dried grass and laid her down gently. When he tried to rise, her arms shot up and pulled him down beside her.

"Oh Lin," she breathed into his ear, her lips caressing his cheek. "I'm mad about you—have been since that first moment I saw you. Take me—take me to Earth III with you."

Her body arched and pressed against his. Her lips slid along his cheek and sought his own, seizing them, pressing into them.

Lin pushed her away, gently but firmly.

"And how would we go?" he asked harshly. "Your half brother had the Indians strip our parachutes and inter-plane belts off us."

"I can get two of them," Mara said. "We can go away, we two, and forget all about Earth V and its troubles, and be happy together."

"Do you really feel that way about me?" Lin asked.

"What do you think?" Mara said with a short laugh. Her lips sought his again. She pulled him over onto her. Her teeth bit playfully into his neck while her scented hair brushed against his face.

His fingers reached up and gripped her hair gently. He pulled her face back until he was looking into her eyes. She could see him now. Her eyes were deep pools of fierce passion, beckoning, inviting, daring. Her lips parted to reveal her firm white teeth and pointed red tongue.

His head dropped towards hers slowly until his lips touched hers again. He kissed her, letting all the passion she had built up in him enter that kiss.

Then, without warning, he drew back and hit her sharply on the side of the jaw.

He felt her go limp under him. Her head lolled back, her eyes turning queerly just before they were covered by their lids. He lifted up on the palms of his hands and looked regretfully at her smooth, incredibly beautiful face. He shook his head slowly in a dazed fashion.

"Lin Carter," he said softly to himself, "you are a fool about scruples." He recalled what Artaxl had said about Mara and her conquests, and what happened to those who fell for her when she tired of them, and felt better as he stood up.

He looked down at her, his brooding eyes taking in her figure, graceful even in unconsciousness. He wondered what she would do when she recovered—if he were still around.

Her dress had been pulled up. He admired her shapely limbs regretfully and bent over, covering them again. Then he turned away from her and went to the door.

He opened it cautiously until he could peek out. There was no one in sight. The fire had burned down to a mass of smoldering embers. He opened the door wider and stepped out, leaving it open.

On the far side of the cavern were sleeping Indians crowded together on grass mats. In the center of the cavern were piled stores of various kinds. He went to them and searched hastily until he found some thin rope. With this he returned to his prison and bound Mara. He ripped off part of his shirttail to make a gag so she couldn't cry out when she awakened.

Satisfied that she couldn't make an outcry for some time after she recovered, he left, closing the door and latching it.

Now the problem was to find Edona and Arthur Gates. He hadn't been able to see where they were taken. They could be in any of the many small rooms opening onto the main cavern—but also any of those rooms could hold Montakotl or some of the other white Incas who might awaken if he looked in on them in his search.

The logical answer came to him suddenly. The doors of the rooms housing the others would be latched on the outside! It would be simple.

Suddenly he remembered his shoes. They were back in the room he had just left. Should he go back and get them? He decided against it. He would have to carry them, and if there were a battle they would be in the way.

He stole cautiously along the wall of the cavern to the next doorway. And the next. Each door he came to was unlatched on the outside, proving there was no prisoner inside.

He went as far as he dared around the wall of the cavern, then returned to his starting point and searched the other way. The fourth door he came to was latched securely on the outside. He pressed his ear against it and listened. No sound came from within.

His hand went to the latch as he turned his head to look over the cavern and see if anyone was stirring. There was no movement anywhere, but at any instant one of the Indians might wake up and see him, and spread the alarm.

Very carefully he lifted the wooden pin that locked the door, and pushed the door open. As he stepped into the room he tried to see. In the feeble light from the smoldering fire in the cavern he made out Edona's white face and staring eyes. She was sitting up, trying to see who was framed in the doorway. There was doubt, fear, and hope on her face.

"It's me, Lin," he whispered.

Instantly she was on her feet and in his arms. He put his own around her—and a deep gladness rose within him that he had not fallen for Mara's charms. He could not help comparing Mara's passionate lust with Edona's clean love.

"How did you escape?" Edona asked after a few moments.

"Mara," Lin said wryly. "Right now she's probably waking up from the sock on the jaw I gave her, and thinking up a million ways to torture me to get revenge."

"I hate her," Edona said.

"Save it, sweetheart," Lin said. "We've got to find that reporter and our inter-plane belts and drop out of here. Any minute it may be too late."

He kissed her tenderly on the lips. As she returned the kiss hungrily he marveled how two hungry kisses could be so different, the one full of unlicensed passion, the other so honest and sincere.

"Let's go," he whispered.

Arthur Gates was three doors away. He was awake, searching for some means of escape. Lin almost got hit as he unlocked the door and stuck his head in. Gates recognized him just in time.

Lin and Edona stepped inside while the three held a hasty discussion.

"We can do one of two things," Lin said swiftly. "We can search for our belts and drop back to Earth III, or we can try to make it back outside the cave without the belts. I think that would be almost suicide—almost worse than being captured again, because without the belts we would never be able to get back down to earth."

"Montakotl would probably have those belts right in his own room," Edona said. "He must know that Mara would want to—"

"Wait a minute," Lin interrupted. "Mara said she could get two of them. Whether she meant our three or another two, she must have had them in her possession in her own room. Do you know where that is, Edona?"

"Yes!" Edona replied eagerly. "That's probably where they are. The two, anyway. Let's look there first."

They went to the door and peeked out. The Indians across the cavern were still asleep. With Edona leading the way they crossed the cavern diagonally to one of the doors. Edona started to open it, but Lin pulled her aside and opened it cautiously himself.

Inside candles were burning brightly, lighting up the room with its elaborate furnishings. Rax had spared nothing to make his wife, Mara, comfortable.

When the three were inside, Lin closed the door and latched it. The three started searching. There were four large rooms. They searched swiftly, knowing that every moment might be their last in which to search further.

They covered all four rooms without finding anything that looked like an inter-plane belt with or without a chute. Finally they had to give up and stand in the middle of one of the rooms, looking dolefully at the shambles they had made of it.

"Wait," Edona said abruptly. "I'm sure she has some secret chambers somewhere, where she stores her jewels. She would have the belts there, where the Indians couldn't get at them."

She went to one of the walls and stooped down, her fingers exploring for movable rock that would start a secret door to opening.

Lin and Art got the idea by watching what she did, and chose other sections of the room they were in.

"Personally I think we're picking the wrong room," Art said after awhile. "She'd be more apt to have secret doors in her bedroom."

"You're right," Edona said.

They left off and went to the room farthest back, where a luxurious bed reposed in one corner.

Almost immediately Arthur Gates gave a grunt of satisfaction and straightened up. Lin and Edona glanced up from their own exploring to see a section of the stone wall moving back.

Shortly it began moving aside, until there was revealed a tunnel. Art took a candle with a proprietary air and entered to look around, turning around with a disappointed expression.

"Only a tunnel," he said. "No jewels. Probably the service entrance to her apartment."

"More likely the way Mara's secret lovers came in," Edona said dryly. "Rax often had the front watched, and wouldn't believe she was untrue to him, because he never caught anyone coming in here that wasn't supposed to."

"No wonder she had them killed," Lin said. "If she hadn't, one of them might have given her secret away. Let's leave it open and keep on searching. There must be a secret room where she hid the belts."

"We have a way to escape now, anyway," Art said.

"But where to?" Lin said skeptically. "That probably just leads to some side tunnel. Unless we find the belts we won't ever get out of here without getting caught. Almost certainly some of the Indians are awake by now. We could never leave Mara's apartment without being seen."

"Unless this tunnel leads to the outside," Art said. "I can't help thinking the bigshots of this world have always had an ace up their sleeve, like a secret way to escape in case of trouble with the Indians over something. I'll bet it goes to the outside."

"Maybe you're right," Lin said, "but let's finish this room and as many of the other three as we can. If anyone tries to come in they'll make some noise and give us a chance to escape through that tunnel."

What seemed like hours later, they stood up in defeat. There was no evidence of any other secret opening of any kind. They looked at one another in despair.

Edona's eyes filled with tears suddenly. Lin took her in his arms.

"My father," Edona said in a muffled voice. "It looks like I won't get to see him."

"You did your best," Lin soothed. "He wouldn't expect you to do more." He glanced meaningfully at Art Gates. "We'd better be going now."

With Art leading the way, he led Edona into the tunnel. Art found the projection that started the stone back into place. The entrance was almost closed when sounds came through that indicated someone was trying to get into Mara's rooms. The sound might have been something else. It was blocked off by the final inch of closing of the stone door.

"Let's go," Lin said abruptly.

CHAPTER THIRTEEN

ART GATES, in the lead, went very slowly, moving the candles he was carrying around while he explored the walls of the tunnel.

"What are you looking for?" Lin asked impatiently. "If that was someone breaking into Mara's rooms, it means she's been found, and will be coming after us."

"That's the very reason I'm looking so carefully," Art explained. "There may be secret doors in this tunnel, leading to secret rooms we can hide in—maybe even a room with those belts in it so we can get clear away."

"You're right," Edona said. She and Lin joined in the searching of the walls, foot by foot. Wherever the walls were rough enough near the floor to conceal the cracks of a movable stone, all three tested them carefully.

Meanwhile the tunnel was curving in a wide arc as though circling the main cavern. For the most part the walls were solid and without flaw, showing veining's of minerals that indicated the original purpose in tunneling so elaborately. The occasional cracks or splits were obviously natural in origin.

The air was dry, a little stale, and when Lin lit a cigarette once the smoke hung motionless, showing that there was no opening to provide a draft.

"Begins to look like there won't be any secret doors," Art Gates commented.

"Let's make a mark on the wall with the end of a candle," Lin suggested. "Then if we search from the other direction we'll know how far we looked from this way. I think we should go on ahead as fast as we can and see where this tunnel leads to."

"Maybe you're right," Art said, "though I feel we shouldn't overlook any bets as we go along. We might pass up a secret room with belts and parachutes in it and run into a reception party wherever this leads to."

"Or," Edona said, "this tunnel might lead directly to what we're looking for. I've been thinking that for some time now."

"It's just like playing poker," Art said with a short laugh. "We can call, raise, or lay down—and until we see the other side of the table we won't know which was the right thing to do. You're probably right though. We'd better just call, by following this tunnel to its end."

He scraped the end of a candle against the wall until it had left a white line a foot long. They began walking, their eyes scanning the walls rapidly in hopes of discovering a secret floor anyway.

Almost immediately they came to a fork in the tunnel. Each fork went off at the same angle from the main stem, so that there was no indication as to which would be the better to follow.

"Where could they go?" Art asked, mystified. He chuckled after a moment. "Reminds me of playing poker where you call, and the guy next to you raises the original bet, leaving you with the conviction you should have laid down in the first place. I don't think our three of a kind, meaning us, is going to win the pot; but we can't back down now."

"Look," Lin said. "The way the tunnel angled off from Mara's rooms indicates that it was circling the main cavern. My guess is that the right fork leads to some secret outlet in the native village, and the left fork leads in the direction of the outer valley, maybe opening at the base of the cliff. That would seem most logical, too, if this is a tunnel to be used to escape."

"Or to meet messengers from Montaca as Mara most probably did all the time," Edona said.

"So let's take the left fork and see if it leads to the base of the cliff outside the canyon," Lin suggested. "Maybe we can get out and intercept the Indians we left coming back to the village. Then we'll have some allies to help us."

"Coming back from where?" Art asked curiously.

"We were on our way here when we dropped down to Earth III and you took us to the Gardena airport," Lin explained. "We did that to save time. The Indians are about due now, in a few hours—if they manage to survive and avoid the winged serpents. They have to walk the distance from Riverside to here."

"O.K.," Art said, "but frankly, all I'm interested in is finding those belts and getting back to Los Angeles. As far as I'm concerned Earth V can keep its secrets."

The three followed the left fork. After a gentle arc it straightened out, dipping slightly. The candles Arthur Gates carried were holding up well, burning slowly. The light they cast sent dancing shadows ahead of them as they walked.

Suddenly they were startled by a sharp sound coming from the rear. They stopped.

"What was that?" Art said in a whisper.

"It could have been a chip of rock falling to the floor," Lin said worriedly, "or it could have been something dropped by someone following us."

"Following us?" Edona asked. "But why would anyone follow us? They would be trying to capture us, wouldn't they?"

"That's what I mean," Lin said in a low voice. "They got through to the tunnel and are after us. We'd better run for it."

Art cupped his hand in front of the candle flame and broke into a slow trot, with Lin and Edona just behind him. Lin glanced back often, but saw no sign of movement in the eerie shadows that stretched into nothing behind them. Once he thought he saw light spring up far behind, but it might have been a chance reflection of their own candles. He couldn't be sure.

Of only one thing was he sure. If they were caught it would be the end. Mara would never be satisfied with anything less than death for all of them for the insult she had suffered of being spurned and knocked silly by a man she had thrown herself on. Her pride would be hurt too much for anything less.

"There's the end," Art grunted, slowing down. Lin glanced ahead and saw a blank wall across the tunnel. His heart leaped excitedly. The blank wall would be the stone door plugging the tunnel.

Edona had already jumped ahead and was stooping down in search of the stone plug that would start the hydraulic mechanism to lift the door out of the way. Her gasp of triumph and her straightening up suddenly indicated she had found it.

Slowly the blank face of rock moved. It was a full minute before a crack of daylight appeared. Lin thought it was the most welcome thing he had ever seen.

Art blew out the candles. The crack of light widened. Soon they could see through. They craned their necks. On the other side they could see a small cavern, perhaps no larger than an ordinary room.

As soon as they could squeeze into the opening they started through, Edona first. As she got through she started searching for the plug that would close the opening again.

Lin came out last. Edona started the closing of the door. Then the three looked around them. The cave was barely a widened tunnel, fifteen feet long and ten feet wide. If it were artificial, great pains had been gone to make it look like a natural pocket in the solid rock.

The opening through which the light came was barely large enough for a person to squeeze through, and was close to the floor.

Art was the first to get down and squeeze into it. His whole body went into it until just his feet could be seen. Then he backed into the cave again and stood up.

"What is it?" Lin asked anxiously, noting the expression on Art's face.

"See for yourself," Art said.

Lin crawled into the narrow passage until his head came out at the other end. He saw what Art had seen, that this was indeed an opening onto the outer valley, but at least fifty feet up the face of the cliff, with no way down except to drop.

He studied the cliff face near the hole without finding any projections that could be used to climb down by. Finally he slid back into the cave. He found Art and Edona searching the cave.

"There might be some rope or something so we could let ourselves down," Art explained. Lin joined the search, but ten minutes later they had to give up. "What now?" Art asked dejectedly. "Back to the other fork?"

Lin nodded. Edona stooped and pressed on the rock that could re-open the stone door. It started to move. A crack appeared around it. Immediately the sound of excited voices came from the other side.

"Close it," Lin whispered urgently. Edona's shaking fingers obeyed. The crack started to narrow once more.

"We're caught," Art said. "They'll open it and get us."

"Not if I keep the closing stone pushed in," Edona said. "That works a plug that lets the water run out of the counterbalance, and if both plugs are open the water just runs through without working the door."

"A lot of good that does," Art said. "We can't go anywhere. Eventually we'll have to give up or starve to death."

"We'd die of thirst long before that," Lin said. "The only thing for us to do is try to drop those fifty feet without breaking any bones, and hide in the woods. Even with a broken leg we'd stand a better chance than being captured again."

"Why?" Art asked. "Maybe they won't do us any harm. Remember, they're in the same fix we are—holed up in there where the flying serpents can't reach them."

Briefly Lin told Art and Edona what had taken place between him and Mara. In spite of his attempt at being casual, he felt uncomfortable and guilty as he went on. Long before he got to the part where he knocked Mara out, Art's eyes widened in comprehension.

"No wonder," he exclaimed when Lin finished talking. "A woman scorned, *and how.*"

"I'd like to get my hands on Mara," Edona said, her eyes flashing. "I'd—I'd—Oh!"

"Another woman scorned," Art said smoothly.

"Oh!" Edona repeated, stamping her foot.

"But I see your point, Lin," Art said. "We'll just have to risk broken bones and torn hide. I noticed the cliff wall slopes just enough so that it might be used to slow our fall if we lower ourselves until we hang by our hands, and then let go, so our clothes slide on it. Fifty feet's a long way though."

"I'll go first," Lin said. "Wait until you see how I come out. If I'm able to walk at all, maybe I can gather up some branches and grass and build up something soft to land on for you two."

He didn't wait for argument. While Art protested, he got down and backed into the hole feet first. Edona got down and watched him, her eyes filled with worry and love and belief in him. He smiled at her. His legs dropped over the end. He was hooked to the edge on his ribs. He worked his arms back until his hands angled on the edge, then let himself down slowly and carefully until he was hanging against the face of the cliff.

He twisted his head and looked down. Now it looked much more than fifty feet. It looked closer to a hundred. But it would be impossible to climb back in even if he wanted to.

Art's head appeared above him.

"You'll make it O.K., boy," Art said soothingly. "Just let your fingers slide off slowly and keep as limp as you can. Use your arms as sled runners against the cliff to keep your face clear."

Lin grinned mirthlessly and followed instructions. He felt himself falling. Somehow his fingers got against the fast moving cliff. His arms jerked in reflex motion. He bounced away from the cliff, turning over awkwardly.

He had no memory of hitting. One moment he was falling, the next he was opening his eyes and looking up at Art's anxious face protruding from the cliff. He moved exploratively, found no broken bones, waved a bloodstained hand feebly, then rolled over and got to his hands and knees, feeling the damp coolness of the soft grass against the hot, torn skin of his hands.

He shook his head groggily to clear his thoughts, then stood up, swaying unsteadily for a moment before the dizziness passed.

"Stay where you are," he called up to Art. "Let me see what I can do to make a pile of soft stuff."

Half an hour later he had accumulated quite a pile of grass and sod at the base of the cliff. Finally he waved an O.K. to Art. Art's face disappeared. A few moments later Edona's legs came into view. Lin started to turn his head away, then watched admiringly as she slid out slowly. When she had come out far enough to lower herself and hang by her hands, she looked down and saw the expression on his face. She colored so that even over the distances separating them her face was a deep red. Lin chuckled, then sobered at the imminence of her jump.

Art's hands appeared above Edona. They came out, followed by his head. He seized her wrists. She let go and dropped until she hung from his outstretched hands. He was speaking softly to her. A twinge of jealousy shot through Lin. It was replaced by anxiety as Art swung her away from the cliff and let go.

His eyes followed her hurtling body. She landed and collapsed too quickly to see if she were hurt. He rushed to her side.

"Are you all right?" he asked.

"Yes," she said, rising. Her face was still red, her eyes half angry.

"You have beautiful legs," Lin grinned.

"You shouldn't have looked," she said, trying to hang onto her anger as it slipped away.

"Watch out below!" Art's voice sounded. Lin looked up and saw him hanging, ready to drop. He picked Edona up and carried her a few feet, then let her down.

"You—you!" Edona protested. She suddenly noticed his torn hands. "Oh, you're hurt," she said, all concern for him. She didn't even turn to see if Art had landed safely, as she took Lin's hands and examined them.

"Let's scatter this stuff so anyone else will hesitate about dropping after us," Art said. He looked at Lin and Edona and saw that they weren't even aware he had landed, so wrapped up in each other were they. Disgustedly he kicked the pile of sod and grass until it was spread out thinly.

As he was finishing, Lin looked up from Edona's ministrations and became aware of him.

"Oh," he said. "You landed O.K., I see. That's a good idea, spreading that stuff out. We'd better get going."

"Yeah, but where?" Art said. "We're right back where we started yesterday, and I'm getting hungry."

"We'll have to hide in the woods and wait for the Indians to get here," Lin said.

CHAPTER FOURTEEN

"THINK WE'RE safe from pursuit?" Art asked. It was an hour later. During that hour they had found enough wild berries to sate both their hunger and thirst. They were now resting near where the Indians must come as they approached the canyon where the village was.

"I think so," Lin said confidently. "Remember, they didn't see the battle of the winged serpents over the village, and don't know that some of them are friendly. They won't dare come out to look for us."

"Maybe you're right," Art said. "What's the setup on all this? Indians, white people with a foreign cut to their faces and wearing strange costumes, flying snakes that are translucent, then simply fade out into nothing in thin air...?"

During the next hour Lin and Edona took turns telling Art all they knew about it. He listened gravely, his eyes lighting up now and then at some thought. When they had finished he remained silent for a long time, digesting what he had learned. Finally he spoke.

"The only thing I don't get," he said, "is this part about Earth III and Earth V. Where's Earth IV? If you just jump from V to III, or III to V, what is there to make you think there's a IV?"

"The inter-plane action is a sort of gravity nullifying in three dimensions," Lin explained. "It doesn't shove you out of the plane you're in, but nullifies the gravity in that plane, and the gravity vectors along the fourth dimension pull you one way or another. Earth IV must be smaller in mass than either V or III.

That way you just jump to the plane with the greater gravity pull."

"It must be smaller than Earth II, then," Art pointed out, "or it would pull you that way when you're below V's surface."

"I never thought of that," Lin said, "but you're right."

"Then if IV exists," Art persisted, "how do they know, since it's impossible to get into it?"

"I think I know," Edona said eagerly. "The Incas have traveled from one planet to another in the Solar System, and on some of the other planets the fourth plane can be gotten into. Then they can look where the Earth's supposed to be and see Earth IV in their telescopes. That must be the way they found out."

"You told me something about there being seven suns and seven planes to the solar system, didn't you, Edona?" Lin asked.

"Yes," she replied. "It was Mara herself who told me about that—when she was more friendly toward me and I didn't know so much about her. According to Inca teachings the universe is infinite in all four dimensions, and the seven planes of matter in our system are just an infinitesimal slice of the fourth dimension, held together by the co-centricity of the seven suns. Mara had said that long, long ago her ancestors discovered a different principle that enabled them to actually travel in the fourth dimension. They took long trips that carried them out of the seven solar planes after the first fraction of a second, so that they must have passed through millions of planes. They found stars shining in all of them they passed through, indicating that the universe extends indefinitely into the fourth dimension of space too."

"What about the sixth plane?" Art asked. "Those flying snakes came from there, you say. Is there a sun and planets in that plane?"

"There's a sun, of course," Edona said. "I don't know anything about the planets in that plane."

"The reason I asked," Art went on, "is that those flying serpents may have originated on some planet in the sixth plane."

"Not necessarily, Art," Lin said. "When we were on Earth I with those three flying serpents, there wasn't any atmosphere, but their wings held them up against gravity."

"What did they beat against then, if there wasn't an atmosphere?" Art asked.

"I think they're made of some kind of electronic matter," Lin said. "Maybe there's an electronic atmosphere that pervades all space, that they fly in."

"Oh lord," Art groaned. "Now we even have other kinds of matter to contend with."

"Maybe we have more than that," Lin said. "We've been like children playing in one little back yard. Now we've found that there's more than we ever dreamed of. We have a whole scale of mesons known to nuclear physics. I think they must be the kind of stuff the flying serpents are made of. If we ever get out of this alive, and back to Earth III, I'm going to get a lot of scientists together to work on this."

"You can have it," Art said. "Me, I'm just going to ask my editor for a nice little job on the sport column, and spend the rest of my life at something safe and sane!"

"I hope you can," Lin said seriously. "But from what I can gather, there're natural gateways between the different worlds. Places where the surfaces come together. Maybe they aren't natural. Maybe the ancient people knew all about the different worlds within one another, and built the gateways. The Incas came into Earth V from some spot high in the mountains down in South America. I suspect there are other gateways here in the United States, at Mount Shasta and Mount Rainier."

"Say!" Art exclaimed. "If that's the case we can go upstate to Mt. Shasta and walk through."

"Sure," Lin said dryly. "And we can always come back the same way. It's a thought, though. We might find that we can't do anything else. But—" He stopped.

Once Lin had been driving his car on an icy road and had seen another car coming toward him out of control. He had sat motionless behind the wheel, knowing that nothing he could do would make any difference. The oncoming car, sliding sidewise at a speed of nearly a hundred miles an hour relative to his own car, had taken off his left rear fender and snapped off the rear bumper. It had been that close.

He had never forgotten how he had felt, faced with a situation where action and even thought are so utterly futile that the mind recognizes it and stops in mid-thought, so to speak.

The soft piping of a flute next to his ear produced the same sort of paralysis as it sounded now. He saw Edona and Art blanch as the blood drained from their faces. He didn't turn his head to see what they were looking at, just above him over his left shoulder. He didn't have to. With some sixth sense he knew just where the winged serpent hovered.

Much later he decided that at that first moment he didn't want to look. Instead, he watched the faces of his two companions, using them for a mirror of thought to guess at what was going on.

He saw the horror in their faces increase against the impossibility of increasing, and knew that the serpent was settling toward him. He anticipated its first cold touch eternities compressed into a second or two before it came.

When it came it was a mere pinpoint touch of living, sentient ice against his cheek. It flowed from that one point into his whole being, seeming to reach into even his toes, and rebound back into him again and again.

Then a dumb amazement possessed him. The sensation he was experiencing was in some indefinable way enjoyable. More, it was delightful and exhilarating, a heady wine in reverse. It was as if a whole nervous system that had lain dormant in his makeup all his life had suddenly found something it could respond to—like the adult African who had seen and felt and tasted ordinary ice for the first time in his life.

Suddenly it ended.

He turned his head up then to look, no longer feeling any horror. The creature, transparent, graceful in every line, hovered above him, its long, sharply pointed bird's beak of slightly whitish transparency pointing at him, its short wings a blur of motion. It was not solid, but merely a structured refraction of the light coming from the leaves and limbs of the trees that could be seen through its body.

The only color was in its eyes. Those eyes were blue, but not like ordinary eyes. They were like two dots of blue sky seen through small breaks in white clouds, shading into nothing and without structure. But even as he looked at them they seemed to film over and fade away.

As he watched, the creature darted upward and away, to hover a short distance down the bank of the stream. Its soft fluting call sounded in staccato notes. Lin watched it stupidly, wondering if it were playing with him before the kill. It darted back to him, touched its beak to the side of his face, then sped away, to pause where it had been before and look back.

Suddenly it dawned on him that it wanted him to follow! Rather than being an unthinking wild creature whose only interest was killing, it was actually behaving like a domesticated dog or cat that wanted him to follow it. Its touch against his cheek still tingled deliciously, sending waves of pleasure through him, as he stood up.

"It seems to want us to follow it," he said, turning to Edona and Art. The utter horror mirrored in their eyes as they looked at him seemed to deepen from his lack of concern over the white spot on his cheek.

"Your cheek!" Edona gasped. Suddenly she threw herself against him, her arms around him. Her lips kissed the spot where the winged serpent had left its mark. "If you're to die I don't want to live," she said frenziedly. He pushed her head gently away.

"I'm not going to die, darling," he said with firm conviction. "This one's friendly. It wants us to follow it. I think we'd better do what it says."

"I think so too," Art growled.

He jumped to his feet and walked toward the winged serpent without looking back. Lin followed, half carrying Edona who was still overcome with grief at the conviction that Lin was going to die the way her father had.

The serpent, on seeing them start, began to fly slowly ahead, looking back often to make sure they were coming, sounding its fluid note in short blasts like a child with a whistle.

After half an hour the strain wore off. Edona had recovered her poise. Her anxious eyes went often to the white spot on Lin's cheek until she satisfied herself that it was disappearing rather than spreading.

At the end of an hour they were happy and optimistic about this new development.

"Either that thing is intelligent," Art observed, "or it's following the orders of someone or something that is. Maybe we'll get out of this plane after all."

Lin watched the direction they were traveling, looking back at the mountain wherever there was a break in the trees. He finally decided they were headed toward the Inca city, Montaca.

"We seem to be headed toward Montaca," he said finally. "I wonder if that's where we're going?"

The sun was high in the sky, its huge red disc looking like a bloated Sun III seen through a mist, when they came to the outskirts of the city. Lin and Edona remembered little about it. They had skirted the city before dawn that other time. Now it was broad daylight.

Then what they had seen seemed ugly and squat. Now it seemed somehow beautiful. The buildings were colored in bright designs that reflected redly.

The air over the city was a flashing mass of motion from what seemed literally to be millions of winged serpents in swift, ever changing flight. Few of their bodies were directly visible. They seemed merely swift movements of some refractive property of the air itself.

And from this moving cloud came a muted mass of melodious sound as they emitted their calls to one another.

Now the one that had led them here lifted its long beak and emitted a clear, high note, as though signaling or calling. And from above came a darting mass of refraction that approached with breathless speed and settled into a swirling dome about the three.

Transparent arrows dove from above in what seemed attempts to pierce this dome of movement. It slowly became evident that the battle they had seen over the village was going on here, multiplied thousands of times.

Their guide was inside the protective dome, darting ahead and returning, its staccato note plaintive and coaxing. They increased their pace, following where it led, walking in the center of a wide street toward the part of the city where the buildings were higher and bigger than anywhere else.

It had some definite destination in mind, Lin was sure. He didn't voice his thought, but speculated where they might be going, and why.

Would they be led before some leader or master—or mistress—of these creatures from the sixth plane? Had the snake mother, if such a creature existed in reality, awakened from her sleep to aid mankind again?

Unconsciously he quickened his pace, taking Edona's hand to help her keep up with him. And over them hovered the protective dome of winged serpents, keeping pace.

They came to the center of the city. Lin slowed his pace. Their guide piped insistently in an obvious signal for him to speed up again.

His feet protested. His shoes were worn through on the soles. His tender feet protested. He noticed that both Edona and Arthur Gates were suffering the same trouble. What was happening around them was too bizarre, too unreal, for them to drop mentally to the level of saying anything to one another now.

The walls of the buildings were covered with strange hieroglyphics that would have delighted an archeologist. The street itself was paved with adobe slabs.

But nowhere was there a sign of life, nor even a corpse. The inhabitants had either fled or were hiding in deep cellars.

Now they were leaving the most settled section. Ahead of them, a mile away, rose the vertical face of the cliff that formed the base of the mountain. Their destination seemed to be the base of the cliff now that they were past the large buildings.

The section they were going through was mostly one or two story buildings, much older, laced with cracks that had been patched and patched repeatedly. Some of the buildings had obviously been deserted for a long time, and occasionally they passed one that had caved in completely.

From the indications it was evident that over the years the dwellers had gradually moved their city away from the cliff toward the plains.

The last quarter of a mile to the base of the cliff was a strip of complete wreckage, of buildings that had fallen from age and abandonment alone. It was as if the natives had grown to fear living so close to the cliff, and had moved reluctantly back.

But all this Lin saw with only half an eye. His attention, the attention of all of them including the guide and its companions that formed the protective umbrella, was fixed on what was happening up above.

The aerial battle had shifted slowly, keeping pace with them as they walked through the city. As they came to the half mile strip of ruin bordering the cliff, the battle changed its design with suddenness.

The barrage of diving enemy serpents that had kept their shield busy stopped, as at a signal. At the same instant a large segment of the aerial swarm darted toward the cliff.

From the excitement and alarm that crept into the piping note of our guide and his companions Lin guessed that the enemy had moved to prevent them from reaching their destination, wherever it was.

Lin stopped, so startling were the implications of that maneuver. It was as if he had gone lion hunting and suddenly come upon a mother lion knitting a sweater for her offspring. He should have guessed that the formation that hovered over their heads was a design that could be executed only by intelligent beings. He hadn't thought about it.

Now, suddenly, he realized that these semi-invisible winged serpents from the Sargasso Sea of the sixth plane were as intelligent as humans, at least. And it was a shock.

He stood there, letting the realization soak in, while Edona and Art looked at him curiously, not having discovered it yet for themselves.

The implications soaked in, one by one. He weighed them, tested them, built up a picture of the purposes behind the conflict as they seemed to him.

The guide had turned and was watching him from its position ten or twelve feet above the ground. Its eyes were small dots of blue sky through white clouds again. Its long, slim beak was a plastic fencer's sword held at ready. It seemed to be sensing the change in him. Suddenly he decided to speak.

"Come here," he said to the winged guide.

Immediately it darted down, to hover just in front of him. Its beak reached out and touched his cheek again in a gesture suggestive of a mother touching a child to see if it was all right.

He looked into those two pools of sky that were its eyes. He tried to sense the mind that lurked there, but it was too strange, too inhuman. Even the eyes were not eyes in appearance.

"Can you understand what I say?" he asked. "If you can, give one short sound."

The winged serpent dipped its beak, emitting one soft note. It had understood. Whether it understood the words—which seemed improbable since they were in English—or it had sensed the meaning of the thoughts behind them, it had known what Lin said.

CHAPTER FIFTEEN

"IT UNDERSTOOD YOU!" Edona exclaimed. "Do you suppose it can think with intelligence like a human being, Lin?" There was eager hope in her voice.

The guide emitted another short note that seemed to almost carry a snorted, "Of course!" in it. Its eyes filmed to milky white. It turned its back on the humans to watch the progress of the battle.

"I think," Lin said, looking at Arthur Gates, "that we may get back home to Los Angeles eventually after all."

"I'll believe it when it happens," Art said. "I see what you mean, though. It's utterly fantastic, but that thing undoubtedly understood you. Think we could ask it some questions and get any answers from it? One toot for yes and two for no?"

"Later," Lin said. "I think we're going to have some action in a minute from the looks of things."

The guide was behaving nervously, studying the seething atmosphere between them and the cliff, and turning its head to glance at Lin often.

"Will you want us to run when we start?" Lin asked it. At its single note signifying yes, he added, "Give us three notes as a signal to start." The winged serpent sounded a single note again, and devoted its full attention to what was going on ahead.

Lin took Edona's hand and told Art to grab her other, so that they could run fast when the time came. He winced at the pain of the raw spot where his fingers had been shredded by scraping the cliff as he slid down back where they had come out from the cavern at the village.

The protective umbrella of winged serpents was moving forward slowly. The three humans took an occasional step forward to keep even with it.

Suddenly from ahead came a chorus of notes in a high key, insistent and urgent. The guide serpent uttered three short notes softly.

"Run," Lin said. Side by side, the two men holding onto Edona's hands, they ran, letting the creatures protecting them keep over them as best they could.

Simultaneously it seemed that countless numbers of the almost invisible things gathered before them, forming a flying three-dimensional wedge so dense that it distorted the view of what lay ahead from the multiple refraction of their piled up bodies.

The fluting blended into two distinct tones that, coming from thousands of invisible throats, was almost deafening. The two notes clashed even as the fighting, milling bodies clashed into one another in combat.

Their guide in some mysterious fashion had gathered into itself some cloudy substance that made its form more visible, so that it stood out better in the bewildering pattern of motion. Lin, Edona, and Art kept their eyes fixed on it as they ran.

Strangely, as if from outside his mind, the thought formed in Lin that all this was being seen by light far up in the ultra-violet, light that made the winged serpents' bodies appear opaque and brilliantly colored to one another, and that to the eyes of these creatures the three humans appeared to be shapes of almost unreflecting blackness.

Had the thought come from the guide? Possibly. He didn't pause in his stride as he thought about it.

The notes blasting from the throats of the winged serpents were deafening in this climax to hours upon hours of battle. They echoed from the face of the cliff, now towering higher than eye could see.

Edona was crying out from the pain of bruised feet, but Lin urged her on unmercifully, knowing that seconds were precious as the enemy creatures made an all-out attempt to keep them from reaching—what?

What was their goal that was so important that these intelligent beings would sacrifice themselves in huge numbers to help them reach it, while the others were risking all to keep them from it?

Were they to play some vital role in events to come that only they could play? With part of his mind Lin thought about this. It must have something to do with why the winged serpents were in two camps, fighting against each other. But there was no way to know what it might be. Was one faction determined to rule the worlds within worlds, while the other was determined to prevent that? Even if that were so, what part could three small humans play in such a thing?

Suddenly Lin's thoughts were diverted by something that had been bothering him for several minutes. He had thought the earth was shaking under his feet at each step, but dismissed it as weariness.

Now he saw that it had been shaking. Racing along the bottom of the cliff in wild stampede were creatures so huge that the sight of them made the mind doubt the validity of the image of them.

The enemy forces had brought in their surprise weapon, the Xinli! There was still a hundred yards to go to the base of the cliff, and the Xinli were half a mile away. It would be close, and if they didn't make it, the mere momentum of those hundreds of tons of onrushing flesh of the giant prehistoric creatures would carry them through the defensive attacks of those protecting them.

"Faster," Lin panted.

They ran, punishing their bare feet until they were too numb to feel any sensation.

The Xinli were close. It was becoming almost a certainty that they would run the three humans down. At the last it settled into a race to reach the protection of the opening in the base of the cliff before one of the monstrous mountains of flesh could get to them. Its head was stretched out, a nightmarish thing of scales that reflected the reddish sunlight metallically, enormous teeth of yellowish ivory, nostrils large enough to crawl into, the whole being as large as an automobile and somehow suggestive of one, hoisted into the air at the end of a massive stalk.

That head was over them, directly above. The sun was blotted out. Then they had leaped in one last desperate attempt to reach safety.

Lin felt himself thumped painfully. He found himself flying through the air. By some freak of co-ordination he landed against the cliff on his feet and bounced, to drop to the ground.

He felt himself seized by the foot and dragged. It was Art, pulling him to safety.

Then the three of them were huddling together at the mouth of a cave, watching the thundering stampede rush by. Cavernous throats uttered pathetic, almost sub-audible rumbles of vibration in dumbly questioning protest as one after another of the Xinli swept by, driven by the goading of the winged serpents and the mass panic of the herd.

Huge blocks of adobe masonry were flung upwards by yard-thick pillars of flesh, to shatter into thousands of pieces against the granite of the cliff. Half crumbled buildings were reduced to strewn pebbles in minutes.

Then they had swept past, the thunder and vibration of their passing dying down slowly. Where they had gone was flattened earth and stone, as if some giant steamroller had gone by.

Overhead the almost invisible battle of the winged serpents continued as if nothing had happened to interrupt it. The three humans cowering just inside the overhang of an entrance into the base of the mountain felt to the full their pitiful insignificance in the scheme of things.

"God," Art broke the silence between them. "And to think that if we could move a millionth of an inch in the right direction we could see San Diego and Los Angeles and Catalina Island, and the white line of breaking waves of the Pacific coastline. Why, right here where we're sitting, where that thundering herd just went by, are probably white billows of clouds, floating slowly, undisturbed by what goes on here, in this plane."

There was an insistent fluting at their backs. They turned their heads, startled, to see their guide hovering in the gloom of the entrance to whatever cavern this might be. In the excitement they had forgotten him for the moment.

Now they looked around curiously, examining where they were.

They were standing in an elaborately carved entrance cut from the solid face of the cliff. It lacked beauty, partaking of the same subtle lack that the architecture of the city itself had exhibited. It seemed that everything the Incas made seemed to have a quality of ungainliness about it. Yet the carvings and shaping of the entrance were detailed and elaborately done.

The entrance widened into six narrow portals separated by stone columns. They started walking towards these, went through them, and found themselves in a cathedral-like room of huge dimensions.

If it had once been a natural cavern in the rock, it had been expanded and shaped until all evidence of its natural origin was destroyed.

At the far end, at least a hundred yards across the vast floor, rose a pyramid shaped block, truncated so that on top it was flat. The steep sides of the pyramid were steps from four directions, ending at that small square of surface high up.

The guide was moving toward this slowly. They followed, wondering what place this was. Could it be some cathedral used by the Incas?

About them in the air could be felt invisible movement, as if their umbrella of protection were now close about them, protecting them from unseen attack.

They came to the base of the pyramid. The first step was at least a foot high. Their guide was hovering several yards up the steeply climbing steps, waiting for them to follow.

"Here goes," Lin said tiredly. "Think you can make it, Edona?"

"I don't know," she said, lifting a foot and squeezing it. "The way I feel I'd be too tired to even sleep, if we had someplace to sleep."

"I think we'd better try," Art said. "That fellow is probably trying to get us to a place where we'll be safe for a while."

"Say!" Lin said. "Maybe that's it!"

"Then I'll make it if it kills me," Edona said.

The prospect of rest, at the top gave them renewed energy. Ten minutes of climbing brought them to the top step. They stood there looking at the flat, smooth square of stone, perhaps eight feet square, wondering just why they had been brought up here. There was nothing that might offer protection. There seemed no reason for them to have been brought up here at all.

"What are we supposed to do?" Art asked, outraged. "Sit up here and look at the scenery?"

Their guide was hovering over their heads, uttering soft notes in a coaxing manner. Lin looked up at it, trying to sense what it wanted them to do.

Tentatively he took the last step and put his weight on the blank top of the pyramid. The staccato notes came in rapid fire. He paused and looked up enquiringly.

"Don't you want us to step up?" he asked. Two fluted notes answered him.

"Guess he means no," Art commented. One short note replied.

"Well what do you want us to do?" Edona asked coaxingly.

The winged serpent dropped slowly to the surface of the top. Its body seemed to soak into the stone, slowly, as if it encountered resistance. It went in until it was out of sight, then emerged again. Then it hovered just above the floor, its long beak pointed toward them in Disneyish fashion.

"I get it," Art said. "We're supposed to go through the floor. It must be a trap door that lifts." A high eager note from the serpent answered that he had guessed right.

"But how?" Edona asked.

The steps and the flat tabletop seemed to have no knobs or movable parts that might be instruments for starting a hidden mechanism to lifting or dropping that solid expanse. They searched carefully while about them the air moved with invisible bodies and the partly seen figure of their guide hovered over them.

"Maybe it knows what we should do," Lin said. He lifted his head and looked at the creature. "Do you know how to get in?"

The answer was two short, sad notes.

"How do you like that" Art said, disgusted.

Edona had moved around to the far side in her search. Now she called them over.

"Look at this," she said, pointing.

There were hieroglyphics faintly carved into one of the steps.

"I—I think I might be able to read them," she said doubtfully. "Artaxl taught me quite a bit of the meaning of the ancient symbols used by the Incas long ago, and this place must be at least a thousand years old."

"What do you think they say?" Lin asked.

"It isn't exactly what they say," Edona said. "They say that this is the property of Quexlkotl and his sons and sons' sons. That doesn't say much. But it might in the light of something else Artaxl told me once."

"What's that?" Art prompted.

"He was talking about how cruel Montakotl was to the Indians," Edona said. "I asked him why they didn't rebel and throw him out. He answered that the hereditary ruler kept his power through secrets handed down from father to son, and that once, long ago, the natives had rebelled against an ancestor of Montakotl, and that ancestor had single handed brought out horrible weapons that had destroyed two thirds of the population."

"Then this may be a vault holding secrets belonging to the hereditary ruler," Art said. "That would mean that only Montakotl knows how to open it." He was silent a moment, thinking this over. Then, "Oh, Lord! That means if we got to get in here we'll have to go get him and make him open it."

Lin and Edona laughed at the very absurdity of this. It would be impossible to retrace their steps back to the cavern they had escaped from that morning, and if they did manage to get there they could hope for nothing but capture and almost certain death. But their laughter was cut short with surprise as their guide uttered one plaintive note of agreement.

Art stared up at the winged guide in stupefaction. "That does it," he said. "I give up. I mean it!" There was a shade of hysteria in his voice. "Those—others would bring back the dinosaurs or whatever those things are before we'd gone a mile."

"Don't let it get you, Art," Lin soothed. "We mustn't panic, whatever we do."

"Panic hell," Art said. "I don't know what you two are going to do, but I'm going to lay down and get some rest."

He stepped onto the flat square and, while the guide uttered shrill warning notes in rapid succession, lay down.

For a moment nothing seemed to happen. Then Lin uttered an exclamation of dismay and reached for Art's feet. Edona's eyes widened in horror as she saw Art starting to sink right into the solid stone. His head and upper torso disappeared completely.

Lin had a firm grip on his legs and was trying to pull him back. Edona lent her strength. Slowly Art re-emerged as they pulled him back onto the upper step.

When his face came into view Edona moaned. Lin began cursing under his breath, monotonously. Art's skin was red, as though he had been skinned. His eyes were bloodshot, and stared from his face without the light of consciousness in them.

Blood started running from his nostrils. He didn't seem to be breathing.

Lin bent over him and studied his skin closely in the dim light. Then he clamped his fingers over Art's nostrils and placed his mouth against Art's. His chest convulsed with the effort of forcing air into Art's lungs.

A weird, sucking sound came from within Art's chest after a moment. Lin sank back, exhausted.

Edona, puzzled by all this, looked from Lin to Art. She saw that Art's chest was now moving slowly with breathing.

"What happened, Lin?" she asked.

"This is some sort of inter-plane platform," Lin said between breaths. "He just stuck his head into the vacuum of the sixth plane."

Over their heads a lone, sad note agreed with him. It was answered by a deep groan from Art.

His eyes closed. This brought another groan. His hands shot up and covered his eyes without touching them, in a gesture of agony.

Lin and Edona watched helplessly. There was nothing they could do to help him.

It was a good hour before Art had reached any semblance of himself. He still kept his eyes closed as the lesser of two agonies. Every cell of his body ached, as he told Lin and Edona soulfully every minute or two.

But as his pain quieted down he had another story to tell, of what he had seen during that agonizing experience with his head and shoulders in the vacuum and cold of empty space in the sixth plane.

He had seen such a brief picture that it was little more than a still picture in his memory, but it was revealing. Another battle was going on there similar to the one going on over the city, but with far vaster proportions. From his vantage point he had been in the exact center of a gigantic sphere of swirling winged serpents whose undulating, contorting bodies had glowed with luminous blue light.

Overhead the guide added his fluted "yes" occasionally to some remark, to verify what Art was saying.

"That makes the picture a lot clearer," Lin said when Art stopped talking. "It looks like this slab is a gateway between the two planes something like the weapon of cold. It could easily be. I thought the substance of the surface looked artificial, rather than smoothly cut natural stone. It could have enough of some variation of heavy iron in it to provide the bridge. It's very cunningly done, so that there's just enough resistance to passage so that the air doesn't rush across into the sixth-plane vacuum."

"But then the guide didn't mean for us to go down into the pyramid," Edona said.

"I think he did," Lin disagreed. "There must be some kind of field generator underneath to make it work. Maybe when we knocked all the worlds with that inter-plane drive on Earth it set things off. Montakotl fled to the cavern to his half sister to escape the hordes of winged serpents that came through, and he's the only one who knows how to get down there and shut the field off."

Their guide dropped slowly and touched Lin's cheek. He looked into the blue depths of its structureless eye and knew that he was right.

"It means," he said, "that we have to get Montakotl and bring him here, or force him to tell us how to do what has to be done ourselves, to close the gateway. Until we do this struggle going on will have to continue—or Earth V will be flooded with millions of hostile winged serpents that will destroy everything, and maybe even go through to our own world and kill everything in sight."

The guide rose above their heads again and sounded a lone note of agreement.

"How will we ever make it?" Edona asked hopelessly, her eyes on her feet, caked with dried blood mixed with particles of sand.

"You aren't going to try," Lin said. "I'm going alone. You and Art will stay here."

"No," Edona protested. "I'd rather suffer the dangers and agony of the trip than worry about you, as I would every minute."

"Just the same you're going to stay here," Lin said with finality. "Aside from any desire to protect you by making you stay here, I can get there easier alone, and stand a better chance of survival."

"I think you're wrong, Lin," Art said. "Don't forget that Mara probably hates you now. She won't hate me. I'm a stranger. Maybe she'd even fall for me."

"You're in no condition to go," Lin argued. "You can't even see very good now. Let's see you open your eyes."

Art opened his eyes and clamped them shut again with a defeated groan.

"See?" Lin chided. He stood up.

"No!" Edona protested, rising.

Lin put his arms around her.

"It has to be done, darling," he said softly. "You and Art stay up here. I'll go as fast as I can. Alone, I can even avoid the Xinli if the others drive them toward me."

He kissed her tenderly, wondering if he would ever see her again. He didn't see himself how he would overcome all the dangers of the trip and win Montakotl over to coming back with him—or even revealing the secret of how to open the inter-plane slab and shut off the hidden mechanism that was activating it. But there was no other course open that he could see.

CHAPTER SIXTEEN

BEFORE LIN had traveled half a mile he felt the pangs of loneliness for Edona. There was worry, too. He had left her sandwiched in between two battles, one going on over his head as he trotted back over the path they had come, the other centering about the pyramid, but in the sixth plane. If even one of the hostile winged serpents broke through it could kill her. But on the other hand, where she was she was defended by the full force of the friendly ones.

Arthur Gates was in bad shape, too. Lin hadn't said anything about it, but he knew that sudden immersion in a vacuum can cause all sorts of complications. It was a wonder Art hadn't been killed instantly by the frothing of the blood in his veins. As it was, the rupture of all the little skin veins and cells was equivalent to first degree burn, and the man should be taken to a hospital. In a few hours his skin would crack and bleed, and there might be infection.

Lin increased his stride, ignoring the damage being done to his feet at every step. The guide, partly visible, and the dome of defenders over him, invisible except for their refracting properties that caused distant objects to waver with their movements, kept pace with him.

He started to think of the task ahead of him, then forced his mind to think of other things. Time enough to think of what lay ahead when he came to it.

His thoughts turned to speculating about how that *door* into the sixth plane, atop the pyramid, worked. Was the pyramid a necessary part of its working—or merely ornamental, symbolic of the power vested in the Inca?

In all probability the inter-planar properties of the *door* were due to a mixture of heavy-iron impregnated into the top surface of the slab of stone, or even forming the top veneer of it, since mixture of ordinary atoms would obstruct passage of solid material through it.

It was, Lin decided, a very fine piece of machinery, that *door*. It had been designed so that there was a time lag between contact and passage through, so that molecules of air bombarding it wouldn't pass through but rebound normally. It had had to be that way, or the *door* would have become nothing but a giant sinkhole, draining off the atmosphere of Earth V into the vacuum of outer space in the sixth plane.

The *door* was a machine like an electric transformer is a machine—with no moving parts to wear out. It was built to do certain things and avoid certain other things. That hinted at science in an advance stage of development. A stage where men figure out on paper what they want something to do, and the details of construction that will accomplish what they want; then go ahead and make it that way.

The ancestors of the Incas must have been very advanced scientists. They would have been worth knowing. Their descendents—

Lin frowned. Montakotl—he knew little about him except that he didn't like him. What did he know about him? There had been some sort of trouble long ago that had caused Rax and Artaxl to go into hiding. Rax had been married to Montakotl's half sister, and there was more than a hint that Rax was the other focus of whatever the trouble had been. Had Rax tried to usurp Montakotl—and failed? Or had Rax been the rightful ruler, and been successfully usurped by Montakotl? That would be an interesting angle. Also a bad one—if Montakotl didn't know the secret of closing the *door*. If he didn't, then it was lost forever, because Rax was undoubtedly dead. Lin had seen that winged serpent settle into Rax's form.

Rax was dead and Artaxl was dead. Edona's father was dead. Arthur Gates might die unless he was taken to a doctor before long and given hospital care. He himself stood a good chance of being killed by Mara when he got to the cavern. Maybe the whole world would be full of dead people if the hostile winged serpents got through and defeated the others.

And Edona, poor kid, was perched on top of that pyramid with Art, her father dead, alone, and with no way of ever getting to a place of safety unless he came through with what he was going after.

That pyramid! It was the support for a door into another plane of existence. Could the other pyramids—those in South America and northern Africa, have originally been for the same purpose, but opening into the FOURTH plane? An urgency took possession of Lin. And a feeling of frustration. He wanted to get this all done and get back to Los Angeles so he could make plans for a real study of all that he had seen, yet right now Los Angeles might as well have been in some other star system.

He had retraced his footsteps in returning to the village. While he had been occupied with his thoughts he had covered most of the distance. A half a mile of his way had been across the wide swath the stampeding Xinli had mown through the trees in their mad flight to escape the winged serpents that pestered them like hornets. Climbing over and under fallen trees had slowed him down. He had spent a precious half hour finding where the path took up again.

The sun was behind the mountains as he reached the river. It would be hours before darkness fell, but the shadow of the mountain made things gloomy, intensifying his feeling of loneliness.

Now had come the time to plan a course of action. It was too bad he couldn't return to the cavern through the secret tunnel from Mara's quarters, but it would be impossible to climb those fifty feet of smooth cliff to the opening. He would have to enter through the opening at the village.

Suddenly he remembered that other fork in the tunnel that had seemed to lead in the direction of the village. Could he find where it came out by searching the village buildings against the cliff? He decided to try that before just walking in and giving himself up to the mercies of Montakotl and his half sister.

His guide seemed to agree with his decision. At any rate, it seemed to lead the way as he followed the bank of the river into the gorge, and for the third time in his life leap from boulder to boulder along the stretch where the waters beat against the naked face of the cliff itself. The other times Edona had been with him. This time he was alone, except for his serpent guide and protector.

He reached the stretch leading to the village, where he had met his first Indians. In the background beyond the village the white veil of the falls dropped from far up. Its roar was a constant part of the landscape, as permanent as the cliffs themselves.

Everything seemed deserted as it had before, and this time there was no battle going on in the air over the buildings. Lin recalled that the winged serpent had hovered over him at this spot, giving the first evidence that some of the winged serpents were friendly.

His guide was hovering in about the same place, now. Had it been that one?

"Are you the one I met here?" he asked, looking up into its blue spots that served for eyes.

It emitted a softly subdued, single note. Suddenly Lin felt a bond of friendship for this alien thing. Alien it might be, a creature whose very substance was alien to Earth, but it possessed emotions that were as human as human. It too remembered this spot where it had first met him.

While he looked up at it with new found feelings of kinship, it dropped slowly, and touched its beak to his cheek, sending that pleasure-pain of intense cold coursing through his body.

When it rose again Lin placed his fingers to the spot, restoring circulation. There was a thoughtful light in his eyes. Here was an ally, and he hadn't even considered him or it in his plans. With the guide and its fellows he had a weapon he could use to force Montakotl to do his bidding. He looked up at the creature again.

"I hope you can understand me," he said. "I have an idea."

It answered with one short note, signifying it understood.

"Can you enter the tunnel with me and follow me, and remain completely invisible?" Lin asked. The single note answered yes. "Then this is what I want to do," Lin went on. "I want to enter the cavern where Montakotl is, with all of you along, but not revealing yourselves. I want you to protect me without becoming visible. I may decide on a demonstration of power, and in that case you must do what I speak aloud for you to do."

Another single note, clear and high pitched, was the answer.

"One more thing," Lin said. "Can you paralyze without doing permanent harm, so that if I'm attacked in spite of your invisible presence, you can stop the attack?"

The answer was a long time in coming. When it came it was a hesitant and doubtful single note. It seemed to say, "We've never tried that, but we think maybe we can do it."

"O.K.," Lin said with more confidence that he had felt for some time. "We'll go right in and get it over with, then."

Without a further upward glance he strode toward the village and the building against the cliff that concealed the tunnel leading into the cavern.

Over his head the guide slowly vanished. Anyone who might have been watching as Lin approached would have been convinced that he was entirely alone, though they might have gained an impression of queer distortions in the air around him, similar to heat distortions on a hot, dry day.

He reached the foot of the ladder that leaned against the wall of the building, Aztec fashion, and climbed it. Before he stepped through the opening to the interior of the building he looked at the bridal veil of a falls, then in the other direction where the frothing river rushed out of sight around a bend where the two walls of the canyon seemed to come together.

CHAPTER SEVENTEEN

LIN FELT a strange nostalgia as he stepped into the tunnel and stole forward toward the central cavern, from which the murmured sounds of people drifted to his ears. It reminded him of home when he was small, with his brothers and sisters and mother and father and his two aunts that lived with them. Suddenly he realized that of all those people ahead, in the cavern, the only one who could speak to him or understand what he said was Mara!

About him, pressing close to him, he felt the frigid, unseen presence of the winged serpents. Either it was his imagination, or he was sensing an uneasiness in his invisible companions. It was almost as if—they were afraid. The very absurdity of the idea startled him. He chuckled dryly at it, and was startled by the loudness of the sound. But as its echo died, it was succeeded by a melancholy note resembling a single tone from the cry of a morning dove.

Instantly from the cavern ahead the motley of sound ceased. That single note from the winged serpent had penetrated to that cavern and sounded over the heads of the people there, who had thought they were safe from danger.

It was at that moment, while all eyes were fixed fearfully on the opening to the tunnel that Lin stepped out into full view.

From behind him surged unseen motion that swept past him and out into the freedom of the greater space of the cavern.

Had they been suffering from claustrophobia? Was that why they were afraid? It could very well be. In their natural habitat in the sixth plane they lived in empty space, with no particle of gross matter within a hundred thousand miles. It could be that they suffered claustrophobia, but Lin had an uneasy feeling that it was something else. Something he didn't know about.

For several seconds the Indians and whites in the cavern were paralyzed by the drama of his appearance while the echo of the call of a winged serpent still hung in the air. Then they burst into sound and activity.

Montakotl, at the far end of the cavern, shouted words that sent the Indians surging forward toward Lin, obviously intent on capturing him.

"Stop them!" Lin shouted, partly as an order to his invisible protectors, partly in warning to Montakotl, in case he could understand.

Lin's eyes had searched quickly for Mara without seeing her. Now they swung to the foremost of the advancing Indians, a huge, muscular man of copper skin and somewhat savage face.

This man suddenly threw himself back, an expression of indescribable horror transfixing his face. Simultaneously others of them were doing the same. They stopped abruptly, threw themselves back convulsively against their companions, then fell to the stone floor, writhing in agony.

From the air above them came angry flutings, as from the woodwinds of an orchestra. The others stopped and shrunk back, their coppery skins paling perceptibly.

Montakotl shouted his commands again, but they fell on deaf ears.

Lin strode forward. As he reached the Indians they fell back, parting to either side to let him pass. He strode through them, past them, past the fire around which Indian women cowered, and on to Montakotl who stood, erectly imperious, an angry scowl on his handsome features.

Now Mara appeared from the direction of her rooms. She had evidently been watching from there. Her face was expressionless. Her large blue eyes and dark hair framed the beauty of her face.

Lin's eyes were divided between her and Montakotl, but his heart was pounding painfully. A part of his mind was wondering accusingly if it was for this, to meet Mara again, that he had left Edona stranded atop the pyramid with a helpless Art Gates, while still another part of his mind was denying it with a hotness that cloaked a feeling of lying.

"So you came back," Mara said tonelessly.

Lin's face suffused with red. His throat turned dry and hot.

"Yes," he said. "But for a reason." He sounded stilted and formal to himself as he talked. "Tell your brother that I've come to take him to the pyramid to close the door into the sixth plane."

"You didn't come back—for *me?*" Mara asked, her voice over gentle and soft.

"No," Lin said flatly, tonelessly, his eyes dropping from Mara's face to the even more disturbing contours of her breasts behind their veil of finely woven, cream colored cloth, and from that disturbing vision to the just as disturbing one of her slim waist and curving hips, to give up in defeat and turn to Montakotl.

"Then I won't tell him," Mara said.

"What?" Lin exclaimed, jerking his eyes back to her face. Amazed, he was beginning to realize that Mara, rather than hating him and wanting him dead, was all the more determined to get him. His hitting her had added fuel to the fire of her passion rather than quenching it. "Look, Mara," he said desperately. "This is more important than anything else. The *door* to the sixth plane on top of the pyramid in the huge cavern in the cliff at Montaca is open. It's through that that the winged serpents have come, and will keep coming until it's closed. They're being held back now, but not for long. The door has got to be closed, and your brother is the only one who knows how!"

"Then why should you balk at sacrificing yourself to my love?" Mara asked, her red lips curling disdainfully. "Are you then so selfish as to sacrifice all mankind for the futile love of a child? Is Edona worth that? Or am I so repulsive? I see in your eyes that you are drawn to me against your will." She paused, watching his face archly, then added with just a shade of wistfulness, "Your will is all that stands between us, Lin. It's as strong as mine. But I love you, and I have no scruples against taking the human race into my grave."

"But I don't love you—" Lin protested.

"But you do," Mara interrupted. "It reveals itself in every breath you take, the way your eyes caress my body, the way that vein on your temple began to throb when you saw me."

"But it isn't a holy love," Lin groaned. "It isn't the way I love Edona. It's just—passion. Lust. Your body excites me as I've never been excited by anyone before. But I don't love you."

"You could," Mara said softly. "And unless you swear that you will, I will refuse to tell my half brother why you came. I'll tell him lies that will make him kill you."

Lin glared into her inflexible eyes, trying to keep from noticing how blue they were, how beautifully the lashes draped over olive lids, how perfectly her brows arched to frame them.

A breath of air stirred against his cheek. A touch, cold as outer space, penetrating as wine, made him glance up. There was nothing to see, but just over his head burst a sharp, staccato note. It was a command.

"Et tu," Lin murmured bitterly.

"What does that mean?" Mara asked, her face pale and strained. Her voice was sharp and verging on panic. In that moment Lin realized that she was more than a little mad. It wasn't love for him, nor passion, that was driving her to demand his love or sacrifice her life and that of all people everywhere. It was injured vanity and an ego that had gotten its way since birth.

It was the daughter of an Inca, who all her life had been able to command the hearts of men—and their lives—until she encountered Lin.

"I promise," Lin said bleakly. "When this is over, if I still live, and the winged serpents are again locked behind the *door,* I'll send Edona away and be with you as long as you want me."

Mara looked deep into his eyes and knew that he would keep his promise. For just a moment she was a pathetic, lonely woman. Subconsciously perhaps she had never hoped for Lin to promise. The egomania that had been bred into her from generations of autocratic ancestors had probably hoped that he would refuse, so that her unrequited love could be the force that destroyed mankind.

Yet, if that were so, she could not see herself impersonally enough to recognize that in triumph she had scored defeat. And she too had promised. She turned to her half brother and spoke to him swiftly in words that meant nothing to Lin.

Montakotl listened as she talked. He tried to interrupt her several times. When she stopped he spoke rapidly. Her answer to what he said was surprised, uneasy. He spoke again, defensively. Her retort was sharp, demanding. Anger crept into her face and her tones. Finally she turned to Lin again.

"Montakotl says he refuses to leave this cavern," she said bitterly.

"Then tell him to describe to me what to do," Lin said. "I can close the *door* myself then, without him."

Again Mara spoke to Montakotl, at first calmly, then pleadingly as he shook his head.

"He says he cannot do that without breaking his sacred oath to his father to tell no one but his son and successor to the secret," she said.

Lin opened his mouth to say something. Two short notes sounded at his ear. He had been about to tell Mara to tell Montakotl that he would sick the winged serpents on him unless he gave out the secret. The guide had said no. Why? Did this tie in with the mystery of why the invisible guardians were afraid?

"It is within our pact with mankind that we shall not touch the person of the Kotl," a voice formed in Lin's thoughts with sharp clarity.

So this was what it had been so hesitant about outside. It had not known how to tell him that it could not paralyze Montakotl himself, but only the others in the cavern.

Lin glared into the eyes of Montakotl, who stared back at him with an expression of haughty superiority.

He felt an agonizing sense of frustration and bitterness. Too fast for him to even be aware of the change, the frustration changed to insane anger. He stepped forward and lashed out with a hard fist, putting behind it all the bitterness that had grown through hours of suffering and grueling action.

A sharp pain throbbed in his hand, sending waves into his forearm, as he drew back. In his eyes was a light of satisfaction as he saw Montakotl go down, his mouth a mass of broken flesh, blood, and teeth.

He held his injured fist and cursed monotonously while Montakotl opened his eyes, blinked them slowly then felt gingerly of his crushed lips and loosened teeth.

"Tell him there's more coming unless he goes with me and closes the door," Lin said without looking at Mara.

"Yes, my darling," Mara said breathlessly. The admiration in her voice stabbed painfully into Lin's heart, setting up a conflict of pleasure at her admiration and hate of himself for his pledge to love her.

He watched the fear grow in Montakotl's eyes as Mara spoke rapidly to him. He thought, "What a coward!"

He could understand a lot now. Rax and Artaxl had not been cowards. They had had to hide here in the cavern inside the mountains to stay alive, because the ruler over them was a coward, and like all cowards would always try some underhanded method to eliminate his opposition. The complacent contempt that had been on Montakotl's face was transplanted now to Lin's, mixed with disgust.

Montakotl sat up, still nursing his mouth. He took out a broken tooth and looked at it dumbly, soaking in what it meant. Anger slowly suffused his face.

He turned his eyes up into the vacant air and spoke, his voice slurred by the numbness of his lips. But even before he had finished speaking, Mara was talking, her voice imperious and protesting, her eyes flashing as she looked into the space where they all knew the invisible winged serpents hovered.

Something seemed to close in about Lin menacingly, then withdraw. Fluted notes floated softly, questioningly, in the atmosphere.

Was this part of the pact between the winged serpents and the Kotl, that they would obey his commands? If so, Lin could appreciate their quandary. Pledged to obey Montakotl, they could not keep their pledge without breaking an even graver aspect of it—the guarding of the safety of mankind.

But Mara's imperious intervention had provided them with a way out of their quandary. They could not disobey her either, and therefore they could use the keeping of two solemn pledges to break the third.

Lin held his breath. He felt that everything hung on what Montakotl would do next. He looked into Montakotl's pain clouded eyes, waiting. He thought he saw defiance form there. He took a step forward threateningly and felt satisfaction at Montakotl's cringing reaction even though he sensed the invisible winged serpents close in around him again.

Then Montakotl spoke, bitterly, his eyes turning away toward the floor.

"He says he will go with you," Mara said excitedly. Her face was lit up with happiness. She took a step toward him.

Suddenly Lin felt very sorry for her. Impulsively he closed the gap between them and took her in his arms. She tried to hide her face, but he cupped her chin in the palm of his blood caked hand and lifted her face so that he could see into her tear filled eyes.

When he kissed her it was not passion. Nor was it love. It was compassion. He released her and turned away quickly. She stood where he left her, erect, an expression of frozen wonder on her face as she brushed her lips, where he had kissed her, with softly touching fingers.

Lin bent over Montakotl to help him up. That worthy pushed Lin's arms away and stood up disdainfully by himself, while obsequious Indians came swiftly forward, half stooped over in obeisance, and brushed the dust off his robe.

CHAPTER EIGHTEEN

IT WAS MARA who forced Lin to permit the Indian women to bathe his feet and rub soothing oils into the raw skin. He would have held out against it, obstinately, but she threatened to bathe his feet herself unless he gave in.

It hurt his conscience to receive such treatment while Art waited at the pyramid, in need of a doctor, and Edona waited in need of foot bathing and dressing of torn flesh where sharp stones had cut the soles of her tender feet.

And while Mara directed the women who worked over him, Lin studied her covertly. It was a Mara he hadn't seen before— and probably no one else had either. In place of her bold aggressiveness, there was a tenderness with a hint of sadness. He had previously estimated her age as around twenty-eight, but now she seemed no more than twenty. Her eyes avoided his with what almost amounted to shyness.

He began to wonder if he had been wrong, and he could love her as he loved Edona. At the thought of Edona he felt a sharp pain constrict his heart. How could he ever explain to her about Mara? There wasn't any way. He would have to hide the truth and tell her he preferred Mara. It would be better that way. The hurt would be quick and clean. For her to know he loved only her, while he married Mara, would be to condemn her to a life of lonely suffering.

Lin's shoes, when they were forced on, were welcome pressure holding in his feet. He stood up and walked around, while the throbbing in them lessened.

Montakotl stood sullenly by, waiting for Lin to get ready for travel. A small group of Indians stood near him, also ready. When Lin told Mara he was ready to start, she spoke to Montakotl. His answer was abrupt and sharp. An argument ensued. Lin listened, wondering if the coward had decided to back down again; but when Mara explained, Lin found himself on Montakotl's side for once.

"He tried to refuse to let me go with you," Mara said. "But I'm going."

"No you're not," Lin said quickly. "You're staying here."

"There's no use talking," Mara said with finality. "I'm going. If you won't let me start out with you I'll follow—and run the risk of being attacked by the hostile faction of the winged serpents."

Lin looked at Montakotl and grinned wryly, and gave in. It looked like Mara was one girl who always got her own way.

The soft, almost drowsy fluting of the invisible winger serpents overhead changed to excited clarions as Montakotl led the way across the cavern floor to the cave leaving outside, walking with purposeful stride as if the whole thing was his own idea, and the others were just tagging along.

When they emerged into the open air, it was already night. The Moon, unnaturally small and far away, hung two thirds of the way up in the star speckled blue sky. The roar of the waterfall died down as they left the gorge and made their way into the forest. The night air was refreshingly damp and cool.

Lin glanced upward often. Now and then some bright star wavering, giving away the invisible passage of one of the winged serpents in its silent flight, assured Lin that they were still under the protection of those strange intelligent beings from the sixth plane.

What was the origin of the winged serpents? Why were they divided into two camps, one under some sort of ancient pact to guard the welfare of the human race, the other evidently out to destroy it? Lin moved up to where Mara walked alone, flanked by Indians ready to protect her with their lives.

"Mara," he said, "why are some of the winged serpents under some sort of pact that binds them to protect us? And why are the others determined to destroy us?"

"It goes back a long ways," Mara said, her voice soft and somehow wonderful in the darkness. "I've studied some of the history of it. Long, long ago, our race, the Incas, were more advanced in science than Earth III is today. We had airships that could travel indefinitely without replenishing the fuel. In fact, the power unit outlasted several ships, being taken out of a ship when it wore out, and placed in a new one.

"Then we discovered inter-plane travel, and eventually penetrated the sixth plane—to be almost destroyed by an invasion of winged serpents. A weapon was discovered that could wipe them out completely. There was a final battle during which our men even went into the sixth plane to carry on their destruction.

"The winged serpents sued for peace. The Kotl decided to spare them, rather than wiping them out completely; but he realized that at some future date things might change. In a way he was an opportunist. In another way he was probably the wisest of all the Kotls. He created the *doors* in various strategic places throughout both Earth V and Earth III. These *doors* incorporated the most advanced knowledge of the various planes. They were able to reach into any plane, even through solid matter of an intervening plane, and provide an entry into any plane desired. In a way they are like a modern radio on Earth III, that can be tuned to any standard frequency. In operation they necessarily exert terrific pressures and set up great stresses in the fourth dimension, and so must be solidly anchored to tremendous mass. That's the purpose of the huge pyramid. It's—what do you call it that a heavy and powerful machine is set on?—a machinery base. That, in effect, is what the pyramids are. Bases for the inter-dimensional portals.

"The secret of opening these portals became the hereditary property of the line of Kotls, or Incan emperors, of which Montakotl is the last, right now. And by means of them he could call the hosts of winged serpents to do his bidding, and thus maintain his power, even though all mankind opposed his will. He and all his successors and heirs. In return for the pact that made the winged serpents his warrior hosts at an instant's notice, he destroyed all of the weapons that could wipe out the winged serpents, and killed all the scientists who knew anything about it, so that it could never be duplicated again. The legend persists that he kept one deep in some secret cavern in South America on Earth III, the original home of the Incas, just in case the winged serpents proved untrustworthy in their bargain.

"But over the centuries the *doors* have remained closed. New generations of the winged serpents have sprung up, and they have divided into two camps, one still loyal to their pact, the other denying it. And the ancient weapon to enforce peace is gone."

She became silent as if in thought. Lin walked beside her saying nothing, hoping she would continue.

"I think," she continued after awhile, "that when the *door* is closed this time it will be for the last time. Those loyal to the pledge are too few, and the others too powerful. Our race has long ceased to be the ruling race of the Earths. It will never again be the leader as it was in the days of the pyramids, when the rulers of nations gained their authority from the consent of the Kotl of Atlan, backed by his inter-plane weapons and ships."

"Then the Incas once ruled the whole world?" Lin asked, surprised.

"Not directly," Mara said. "Their science made them all powerful compared to the ignorance of other races. Rather than ruling directly, they chose one of the natives to rule a nation, and backed up his authority with their weapons and ships, even molding public opinion in support of the ruler they chose for a nation, in ways that seemed supernatural to the ignorant populace that didn't suspect the existence of other planes of reality co-spatial, three-dimensionally, with their own.

"But as the population of Earth III increased, and the birthrate of the white Incas declined, it eventually became impossible to hold all the loose threads. One portion of the vast empire after another was cut off. Earth II was abandoned except for a few mines in Earth III accessible from that plane, and its sun, larger and much hotter and more lethal in its radiation than sun IV or V, has played havoc with the tribes of man still living there. Some of them tried taking over where our ancestors dropped off, but their efforts to control Earth III have been ineffectual, and have often been just instruments of expression for sating their own sadistic lusts for power. With the instruments for affecting thoughts and emotions from outside a plane, they have raised up men like the Khan of Asia, Alexander the Great, Hitler, and others. But it gets too complicated for them to control and direct. They lose the threads just as my own ancestors did, and go down in defeat.

"By the time Pizzaro and his men invaded the last of our colonies on Earth III in South America it had already been decided to withdraw completely from that plane and consolidate the remnants of our white race, and those parts of the red race still loyal to us, right here in Montaca. So we didn't oppose his invasion, but rather fought a delaying tactic until we could wall up the portal between the two worlds there. Since then that wall has come down, but it served its purpose in the days of the Conquistadors."

When it appeared that Mara was through talking, Lin asked a question that had been on his mind.

"These weapons that you say they used for molding public opinion," he said. "What were they like? Do you know?"

"I know little about them," Mara said. "I think they were small devices that set up vibrations in the atmosphere of another plane, so that someone just outside your plane could project his voice next to your ear so softly only you could hear it, and devices for exciting different parts of the brain by direct contact through the inter-plane fields, to excite various emotions or to disorganize the mind completely, sometimes even being used to kill in ways that produce heart failure or cerebral hemorrhage."

Lin looked upward at the winking stars and cold, small moon; that moon mentioned in mysterious books as the Dark Moon hidden behind the moon of Earth III. He smelled the clean odor of the trees that loomed like dark sentinels about him as he walked beside Mara, following the silent marchers, and being followed by others behind them.

Montakotl's white, full length robe led the long moving procession, followed by the shadowy forms of the Indians. From far away came an almost sub-audible bellow that sounded very much like the sound a steamboat makes when moving through fog shrouded waters undoubtedly the call of one of the Xinli.

"Did you ever hear of a creature called the 'snake mother'?" Lin asked Mara suddenly.

"No," she answered expressionlessly.

Lin thought over her answer. It could mean she didn't know, or that she wasn't going to tell him. Had Merritt gotten the basis of his story about that creature, and invented the snake mother for the sake of the story? Or had his whole account been actual history, or historical novel?

Shaver at least had come out and asserted that what he said was true. And fantastic as it had been, his assertions of deranged humans from two miles under the earth with their devices that stimulated emotions, killed by heart attack and brain hemorrhage, and whispered in people's ears in voices no one else near them could hear, had been right, though he had never known how it had been done.

He had been wrong in some ways. He had concluded that because those deranged creatures lived two miles below the earth they must live in caves. He had concluded that because their sun was the cause of their derangement that it was Sun III, earth's own sun. The truth of the matter was now obvious.

Those creatures living two miles below Earth III lived on the surface of Earth II, under a glaring sun much hotter and more full of harmful radiations.

But, now, what of Charles Forte and his works? He tried to think of some question he might ask Mara that would provide an adequate answer to Forte's mysterious objects that fall from the skies.

"I'd like to ask one more thing, Mara," he finally said. "I've been thinking this way: suppose I were living on this Earth, and wanted to get rid of something—like the skeleton of one of the Xinli who had died and decayed down to his skeleton. Has Earth V ever used a device that would shift such things into the third plane and let them fall to the surface of Earth III?"

"I suppose so," she answered disinterestedly. "Such a device would be very simple, so it may have been invented and used. However, I've never heard of it."

After a few moments of silence she took up the theme again.

"Actually, there's always a certain amount of inter-plane transfer," she said. "Most of it is individual atoms going over, or individual electrons."

Lin was satisfied with the answer. He now had a general picture of the whole, of worlds within worlds, the strange and unbelievable happening overhead in the sky, or in the ground underfoot, but in other planes of hyperspace in a sort of laminated universe.

What caused the universe to collect into hyper-plane laminations that lay against one another loosely would be a problem that might very well be the opening wedge into the basic structure of reality. But beside that, there were the vast new fields of immediate study as the paths of discovery of the ancestors of the Incas, the Atlans, were retraced. And there were the two vast worlds that could be opened for settlement and exploration, not to mention space travel that needed no fuel for escape from the clutches of gravitation, accomplished by merely sliding into a plane of weak gravity, above Earth I—if there were still an Earth I of any kind.

Now, however, the immediate problems that faced them were coming up. Montaca was just ahead. The stars in the sky over the city were in boiling motion from the refraction of invisible bodies by the thousands in combat.

CHAPTER NINETEEN

LIN STUDIED the boiling sky with a feeling of growing apprehension. There seemed many times more combatants now than there had been before. Has some of the enemy burst through the spherical fronts of defense about the *door*, in the sixth plane? If they had, had they killed Edona and Arthur Gates?

He was filled with bitter self-condemnation. He could have seen Edona and Art to a safer place before leaving them, instead of leaving them right at the portal through which the enemy would come. But if the worst had happened it was too late now.

Their own umbrella of defenders was being rapidly augmented until even the path on which they walked wavered and changed direction visually. A chill breath of outer space heralding the close passage of one of the invisible guardians became a commonly recurring thing. The Indians might have bolted if they had been able to find a direction free from the boiling in the atmosphere. Montakotl was held up by a muscular red man on either side, and whether it was from weakness from the blow Lin had given him, or abject cowardice, there was no way to tell from the back of his head.

Lin moved closer to Mara to shield her from the close proximity of the winged guardians as they pressed around them. She seemed to suddenly become aware of his nearness, and moved away, keeping her face half averted.

Why had she done that? What had come over her since Lin had given her his word that he would marry her when the *door* was shut and the winged serpents were gone? He shook his head slowly in bewilderment over her behavior, deciding that now that she was sure of him she had changed to the defensive—like a woman. That thought brought a smile to his lips in the darkness.

The procession was in one of the streets of Montaca. The buildings stood out as solid shadows in the feeble light of moon and stars. Seeming to loom directly in front of them, but also seeming to be incredible miles away yet, the face of the cliff base of the mountain formed a background, a backdrop to the titanic struggle going on. In the darkness Lin discovered that a mortally wounded and dying winged serpent glowed with soft incandescence as it fell, to dissolve into nothingness. It seemed to be the life structure that held it together, and once that was gone the delicate components of its body were unable to resist the pounding of the dense atoms of the atmosphere.

More and more dying fighters came into incandescent view, falling like glowing ever-fire, as the enemy made their all-out attempt to get at Montakotl, the only living being who could close the *door* to their native plane.

And Montakotl, knowing that he was the center of the raging battle, cringed and shrunk from it. It filled Lin with amazement that any man could go to pieces so completely and so unashamedly.

But now another thought came to Lin. Even if the *door* atop the pyramid were closed, how would those of the enemy trapped in the fifth plane be disposed of? When their escape was cut off, might they not flee to some hiding place and bide their time until the defending winged serpents were gone? For surely the defenders wouldn't want to stay after the *door* was closed forever.

Out of the darkness Lin felt a chill touch against his cheek. He looked above him but could see nothing tangible. Still, that touch proved to him that his guide was still with him, near him.

Had that touch been to reassure him that everything would turn out all right? Lin more than suspected that the winged serpent read his thoughts, rather than his spoke words.

The fluting notes of the battling creatures, of all tones and loudnesses, filled the air with deafening musical sound. There was in addition an electrical tension that Lin could feel at the roots of his hair, and could see in the electric sparks cast off by the moccasins of the Indians near him as they walked.

Moment after moment the drama being enacted continued with unabated suspense, huge beyond words to describe, magnificent beyond the ability of camera to record, fantastic beyond the wildest imaginings of human thought.

The procession came to the strip of ruin that lined the base of the cliff where the Xinli had lain everything flat in their blind stampede, goaded by the enemy winged serpents.

Lin left Mara and pushed past one after another of the Indians until he was beside Montakotl. The slobbering whimpers that came from the last spoiled member of perhaps the noblest line of all humanity sickened Lin.

He pushed past that quivering mass of cowardly flesh supported by stoic Indians, and went on alone, feeling the close presence of a thick wall of guardians go with him.

He reached the entrance to the gigantic auditorium chamber within the cliff where the pyramid squatted. He stood there, motionless, for a long moment, trying to adjust his eyes to the deep darkness. He could *hear* motion that filled the cavernous darkness. The soft whisper of beating wings so tenuous that they could not be felt.

He tried to reach out with psychic senses and contact Edona. Suddenly he was filled with an overwhelming conviction that she wasn't there.

"Edona!" he called, his voice sharp with panic and fear for her safety. "Edona!"

The sound of his voice echoed with unabated force, and re-echoed and re-echoed in moronic madness, adding to his feeling of depression and panic.

"Edona!" he called again, his voice being taken up by a gallery of sadistic hecklers and thrown back to him.

Then softly came the touch of ice against his cheek, sending waves of frigid stimulant through him, soothing his frantic mind, restoring partial calm.

"Come." The word formed in his mind with crystal sharpness.

Slowly, before his eyes, the form of the winged serpent materialized, dimly visible with faint, iridescent, slowly swirling substance.

It moved away from him toward the right, away from the direction of the pyramid. With his new found calmness Lin followed, while faintly, from far away, the last faint re-echoes of his frantic call came to him as a mournful, whispered, *"Edona..."* A muted cry of sad despair in the formless void that held Lin suspended in a spaceless nowhere, even while his feet clicked loudly on the stone floor over which he walked, following the spectre that floated before him.

His footsteps echoed loudly as he moved deeper into the darkness after the guide. When it paused he stopped until it moved forward again. When it moved faster he hastened his steps to keep up with it, wondering if its erratic progress were due to the tides of battle going on unseen around him, or because it wasn't sure of which way to go.

When it stopped for the last time it sounded a series of rapid, soft notes that went up the scale in a key no musical instrument had ever captured.

Lin stepped forward, hands outstretched in the utter darkness, and encountered the unyielding surface of a wall.

"Edona?" he whispered hoarsely.

"This way, Lin," her voice answered him.

"Thank God!" he exploded in relief, turning in the direction from which her voice seemed to have come. Directly beneath the softly florescent cloudiness of the winged serpent his searching hands encountered a break in the wall. As they groped slowly forward he felt one seized.

"Lin..." Edona's voice sounded happily.

Her hand drew him forward. He felt her body against him and wrapped it in his arms, feeling her arms steal around his neck as her warm breath fanned his cheek.

For a long instant he held her tight, while the past and the future were washed away by her tears of happiness as she alternately cried and laughed, her soft hair cushioning his chin as she pressed her face against his chest and clung to him, gaining courage and strength from his presence.

Then the echo of other footsteps penetrated consciousness, bringing Lin back to a realization of the present—Montakotl had entered the cavernous cathedral—and with him, Mara!

The remembrance of his pledge to Mara hit Lin with a sharp pain. Tenderly he tried to push Edona away. She stood beside him while they turned to look across the floor to the shadowy outline of the entrance portals where Mara and Montakotl stood out visibly in their white robes, with dark figures flanking them.

"It's Montakotl," Lin explained in a whisper. "He's come to close the *door.*"

Edona put her arm around his waist and stood close beside him, not replying. Together they watched as the two white forms moved into the cavern in the direction of the pyramid.

When they reached a point Lin judged to be halfway to the base of the pyramid they came to a stop. A moment later they seemed to sink into the floor, vanishing from sight.

"A trap door in the floor," Lin whispered excitedly. "We could never have found it in a million years."

They stood tensely, waiting. Lin wondered how the enemy winged serpents would be forced to go back into their own plane. It would not be enough to merely close the door—or would it? Could it be that the guardians were planning on bringing in enough re-enforcements through the *door* to capture the rest of the enemy and force them back where they belonged?

A sound as of a sigh floated to Lin's ears through the medley of fluted calls of invisible fighters. It was as the sigh of a winter wind around the eaves of a deserted house.

Lin felt the moisture on his skin turn to chill frost. A voice sounded in his mind, compelling, demanding.

"Back," it said. "Get back as far as you can and get down flat on the floor."

From Edona's sudden movement the same voice must have formed in her own mind. Together they lay down, hugging close to each other.

The deep sigh grew stronger, more throaty. A roaring thunder was born in the sound and grew and grew until it blotted out all other sounds.

A sharp pain came suddenly in Lin's ears. He opened his mouth and felt relief.

The atmosphere around him was in motion. The luminous form of the winged serpent that had been his guide started to fade into nothingness, but even as it faded it seemed to be seized by some gigantic hand and pulled away in the direction of the pyramid.

And now atop the pyramid a line of glowing light, a square shaft of light, began to appear in the total darkness. It was as if a door had been opened into a dimly lighted room. In the rays of that square, outward fanning shaft of light, an undulating madness of shifting movement grew, going downward into it, swifter and swifter.

The roaring grew louder, and the louder it grew the swifter the swirling, seething motion became, until it was just a blur.

From the direction of the entrance into the cavern: from the outside came a moaning sound, as of wind whistling through trees in a forest. Loud crashings told of solid objects being hurled against the cliff, and of debris thrown into the cavern to land, shattered, against the stone expanse of the floor.

"Goodbye." It was a faint voice forming in Lin's mind from far away, with a hint of sadness and finality.

"Goodbye." Lin formed the word in his mind, and shaped it with silent lips, knowing that his friend from another dimension was gone, forever.

Now the entire mountain seemed to be trembling with some strange force more gigantic than that of stampeding Xinli. The roaring vibration increased to a thunder, as of a thousand locomotives blowing steam in the night.

The boiling in the square shaft of light atop the pyramid lessened until it was no more. The light reflected from the vast dome of the cavern, revealing huge chunks of stone breaking free and falling to the floor with loud reverberations.

Lin's mind had long ago penetrated to the nature of the force that had been unleashed. It had been ultimately simple. From the controls under the pyramid where Montakotl had gone, he had merely tuned the door more sharply, so that the sixth plane was wide open, allowing the atmosphere of Earth V to rush through it into the vacuum of outer space.

That *door* had become a wide open valve, with perhaps a hundred square feet of opening, through which the air was rushing unimpeded, and dragging everything with it that could come loose.

Even in the protected cubbyhole where Lin and Edona lay it threatened to pluck them loose and carry them along.

But now the whole roof was caving in, with huge blocks of stone crashing down. Like something unreal, gigantic blocks were falling into the maw of the doorway into the sixth plane.

Abruptly the roaring thunder stopped, to be succeeded by a silence as deep. For one cosmic instant the square shaft of light over the pyramid stayed. Then it vanished.

From deep under the pyramid, under the thousands of tons of rubble that covered the floor of the cavern, Montakotl had closed that portal into the Sargasso Sea of the sixth plane. Closed it forever.

CHAPTER TWENTY

LIN GLANCED over the edge of the plane. It was the new test model of the XB56, officially designated as the XB56IPD. To the south the mountainous topography of San Diego stretched to where the dim tongue of the bay of lower California could just be seen. To the north sprawled the vast area of Los Angeles.

Underneath the plane was the erratically traced white line of the shore of the Pacific where its waves broke against the eternal solidity of California. And to the east, but so far below that they appeared to be little hills, were the mountains that walled in the coast from the deserts of eastern California and Nevada.

He settled back in the pilot seat, a boyish smile on his lips as he turned his eyes to the blond head close to his shoulder. His hand shot out, his fingers touching lightly on the plastic handle of a lever on the dash.

"Here goes, darling," he said lightly. His fingers constricted, pulling up on the lever. Nothing inside the plane changed.

But outside, the earth abruptly jumped up so that the plane was barely skimming a thousand feet above treetops, and to the west rose the vertical cliffs of a mountain that rose far above the plane.

"How does it feel to be riding in a plane designed by your husband, Mrs. Carter?" Lin said.

Edona pouted her lips in simulated study. "Oh," she hesitated, "a little tame, to tell you the truth."

"Tame she says," Lin groaned. He turned his head and looked entreatingly at Arthur Gates who returned his gaze with a philosophical shrug and a quiet smile tugging at the corners of his mouth. "Do you suppose I've gotten myself attached to one of these female adventurers who will keep me hopping from one mad adventure to another for the rest of my life?"

"Not me," Edona said quickly. "I'm the home type. All I want for Christmas is my two front steps—and a door leading into a warm, cozy home where I can live for the rest of my life."

"Then what are you complaining about," Lin said with feigned indignance. "Didn't I buy you one the minute we were married?"

"Just out of this world," Edona sighed, settling back in her seat dreamily.

"I should hope so," Lin said, looking out at the scene below.

They were over the city of Montaca on Earth V. Below were small dots moving slowly along the straight lines that were the streets.

To the right rose the cliff base of the mountain, uninterrupted except for a gaping hole where the giant cavern cathedral had been.

His face sobered at the sight. Somewhere in there, buried under hundreds of tons of fallen rock from the caving in of the ceiling, lay the body of Mara.

She must be dead, he thought. Even if she had survived, she would have died of starvation and thirst by now. It had been two months since that awful night when the very foundations of a world had seemed to tremble, and the whole mountain had threatened to fall in on them.

They had lain there waiting for the dawn, and when it came it revealed the mountains of shattered rock over which they had climbed painfully to safety, to make the slow journey back to the village and search until they found their inter-plane belts and parachutes, and drop down to Earth III and home.

He had kept silent about his pledge to Mara. If she were dead there would be no reason to tell Edona. Time enough for that when she appeared, alive. But she never would now. Lin felt sure of that. If she did—

"You know," Arthur Gates said, "I sort of wish that cave-in hadn't sealed up Mara and probably killed her… I think I could go for that girl if she were alive. The trouble with her was that she didn't have a chance. She could probably count the eligible males in Montaca on the fingers of one hand from the time she first became aware there were men. She never had a chance to meet a nice guy like me."

"She was an unscrupulous cat," Edona said, looking queerly at Lin. "I'm glad she's dead, in a way. Maybe I'd have had trouble with her if she'd lived."

"About me?" Lin asked in mock amazement. "Don't you know me better than that?"

"I do," Edona said skeptically. "You never have explained why you didn't sock Mara the minute she came into the room where you were locked up instead of waiting and giving her a chance to throw herself at you."

"Do I have to explain?" Lin asked teasingly, hiding the look in his eyes at this reminder of something that still lay in his heart against his will. Edona looked at him, the light of love in her deep blue eyes almost a visible beam.

"No, darling," she said softly. "That is, you don't have to if you let me take the controls for a while."

Groaning in simulated defeat, Lin slid over while Edona took the controls.

"Look out!" Art shouted from the rear seat as the needle nose of the plane tipped down in a vertical fall.

But suddenly Earth V vanished and Earth III appeared two miles below as she flicked the inter-plane drive lever.

"Ohhhhh," Art moaned as the plane screamed downward at a speed bordering on supersonic.

And Earth III vanished, to be replaced by Earth II.

"That's enough," Lin warned quickly. "We don't know what lies in the first plane now—and we're through taking chances for a long time yet."

Edona brought the plane out of its dive and leveled off. As Lin took the controls again she slid over, blinking her eyes against the blinding sun.

"Take me home, Lin," she said meekly.

The three were silent as the long nose of the plane lifted toward the giant sun and the bleak surface of Earth II dropped away.

Far below, distorted creatures whose ancestors had been men lifted vacuous faces toward the direction from whence the soft roar of jets had originated, while eyes, made sightless from birth by the overabundance of ultraviolet rays from Sun II, instinctively moved as though searching for the source of the sound—a sound they would hear again, and again, until the races of Earth III came to rescue them, as the inter-plane drive came into usage and the peoples of Earth began their great expansion into that greater universe of worlds within worlds, that formed a four-dimensional stairway leading to the stars.

THE END

ALIEN SLAVE SHIPS OVER EARTH!

It seemed unimaginable that scores of alien spaceships had been coming and going from Earth, virtually undetected, for centuries. Even more unimaginable was the fact that these alien vessels had been taking with them untold thousands of human beings who were transformed into pitiful galley slaves, used for driving their captors' spacecrafts from one side of the galaxy to another.

When agents of Earth finally became aware of their planet's plight, it was decided that one agent would be sent in, and it must be an agent with extraordinary mental powers—far above those of the average human. The only problem was that the agent selected was a washout with the service and now a wandering bum with a propensity for too much booze!

CAST OF CHARACTERS

CHUCK BARKER
A drunk, a total washout. Yet his actions (or lack thereof) might well determine the fate of the human race and the planet Earth.

DR. OLIVER
This professor of languages had a terminal medical problem and he'd do anything to save his life. But who was he really?

OLD MAN STOSS
Everybody loves a kind-hearted swindler, and this old con-artist's abilities at slight of hand proved invaluable.

LAKHRUT
A walking alien cyclops, as cold-blooded as they come and not afraid to inflict mind-numbing pain on his galley of Earth slaves.

BALDWIN
He was bull-necked and coarse in personality with a streak of cruelty. Worst of all, he was a traitor to his own race.

GINNY STOSS
She was a beautiful Earth girl. But the aliens had rendered her a nearly mindless, muttering galley slave.

THE SLAVE

By
C. M. KORNBLUTH

ARMCHAIR FICTION
PO Box 4369, Medford, Oregon 97504

CHAPTER ONE

THE DRUNKEN BUM known as Chuck wandered through the revelry of the New Year's Eve crowd. Times Square was jammed with people; midnight and a whole new millennium were approaching. Horns tooted, impromptu snake-dances formed and dissolved, bottles were happily passed from hand to hand; it was minutes to A.D. 2,000. One of those bottles passed to Chuck and passed no further. He scowled at a merrymaker who reached for it after he took his swig, and jammed it into a pocket. He had what he came for; he began to fight his way out of the crowd, westward to the jungle of Riveredge.

The crowd thinned out at Ninth Avenue, and by Tenth Avenue he was almost alone, lurching through the tangle of transport machinery that fed Manhattan its daily billion tons of food, freight, clothes, toys. Floodlights glared day and night over Riveredge, but there was darkness there too, in patches under a 96-inch oil main or in the angle between a warehouse wall and its inbound roofed freightway. From these patches men looked out at him with sudden suspicion and then dull lack of care. One or two called at him aimlessly, guessing that he had a bottle on him. Once a woman yelled her hoarse invitation at him from the darkness, but he stumbled on. Ten to one the invitation was to a lead pipe behind the ear.

Now and then, losing his bearings, he stopped and turned his head peeringly before stumbling on. He never got lost in Riveredge, which was more than most transport engineers, guided by blueprints could say. T.G. was *that* way.

He crashed at last into his own shared patch of darkness: the hollow on one side of a titanic I-beam. It supported a freightway over which the heaviest castings and forgings for the city rumbled night and day. A jagged sheet of corrugated metal leaned against the hollow, enclosing it as if by accident.

"Hello, Chuck," T.G. croaked at him from the darkness as he slid under the jagged sheet and collapsed on a pallet of nylon rags.

"Yeh," he grunted.

"Happy New Year," T.G. said. "I heard it over here. It was louder than the freightway. You scored."

"Good guess," Chuck said skeptically, and passed him the bottle. There was a long gurgle in the dark. T.G. said at last: "Good stuff." The gurgle again. Chuck reached for the bottle and took a long drink. It was good stuff. Old Huntsman. He used to drink it with—

T.G. said suddenly, pretending innocent curiosity: "Jocko who?"

Chuck lurched to his feet and yelled: "Damn you, I told you not to do that! If you want any more of my liquor keep the hell out of my head—and I *still* think you're a phony!"

T.G. was abject. "Don't take it that way, Chuck," he whined. "I get a belt of good stuff in me and I want to give the talent a little workout, that's all. You know I would not do anything bad to you."

"You'd better not... Here's the bottle."

It passed back and forth. T.G. said at last: "You've got it too."

"You're crazy."

I would be if it wasn't for liquor...but you've got it too.

"Oh, shut up and drink."

Innocently: "I didn't say any thing, Chuck."

Chuck glared in the darkness. It was true; he hadn't. His imagination was hounding him. His imagination or something else he didn't want to think about.

The sheet of corrugated metal was suddenly wrenched aside and blue-white light stabbed into their eyes. Chuck and the old man cowered instinctively back into the hollow of the I-beam, peering into the light and seeing nothing but dazzle.

"Look at them!" a voice jeered from the other side of the light. "Like turning over a wet rock."

"What the hell's going on?" Chuck asked hoarsely. "Since when did you clowns begin to pull vags?"

T.G. said: "They aren't the clowns, Chuck. They want you—I can't see why."

The voice said: "Yeah? And just who are you, grampa?"

T.G. stood up straight, his eyes watering in the glare; "The Great Hazleton," he said, with some of the old ring in his voice. "At your service. Don't tell me who you are, sir. The Great Hazleton knows. I see a man of authority, a man who works in a large white building—"

"Knock it off, T.G.," Chuck said.

"You're Charles Barker," the voice said. "Come along quietly."

Chuck took a long pull at the bottle and passed it to T.G. "Take it easy," he said. "I'll be back sometime."

"No," T.G. quavered. "I see danger. I see terrible danger."

The man behind the dazzling light took his arm and yanked him out of the shelter of the I-beam.

"Cut out the mauling," Chuck said flatly.

"Shut up, Barker," the man said with disgust. "*You* have no beefs coming."

So he knew where the man had come from and could guess where the man was taking him.

AT 1:58 A.M. of the third millennium Chuck was slouching in a waiting room on the 89th floor of the New Federal Building. The man who had pulled him out of Riveredge was sitting there too, silent and aloof.

Chuck had been there before. He cringed at the thought. He had been there before, and not to sit and wait. Special Agent Barker of Federal Security and Intelligence had been ushered right in, with the sweetest smile a receptionist could give him...

A door opened and a spare, well-remembered figure stood there. "Come in, Barker," the Chief said.

He stood up and went in, his eyes on the gray carpeting. The office hadn't changed in three years; neither had the Chief. But now Chuck waited until he was asked before sitting down.

"We had some trouble finding you," the Chief said absently. "Not much, but some. First we ran some ads addressed to you in the open Service code. Don't you read the papers anymore?"

"No," Chuck said.

"You look pretty well shot. Do you think you can still work?"

The ex-agent looked at him piteously.

"Answer me."

"Don't play with me," Chuck said, his eyes on the carpet. "You never reinstate."

"Barker," the Chief said, "I happen to have an especially filthy assignment to deal out. In my time, I've sent men into an alley at midnight after a mad-dog killer with a full clip. This one is so much worse and the chances of getting a sliver of useable information in return for an agent's life are so slim that I couldn't bring myself to ask for volunteers from the roster. Do you think you can still work?"

"Why me?" the ex-agent demanded sullenly.

"That's a good question. There are others. I thought of you because of the defense you put up at your departmental trial. Officially, you turned and ran, leaving Jocko McAllester to be cut down by the gunrunners. Your story was that somehow you knew it was an ambush and when that dawned on you, you ran to cover the flank. The board didn't buy it and neither do I—not all the way. You let a hunch override standard doctrine and you were wrong and it looked like cowardice under fire. We can't have that; you had to go. But you've had other hunches that worked out better. The Bruni case. Locating the photostats we needed for the Wayne County civil rights indictment. Digging up that louse Sherrard's wife in Birmingham. Unless it's been a string of lucky flukes, you have a certain talent I need right now. If you have that talent, you may come out alive— and cleared."

Barker leaned forward and said savagely: "That's good enough for me. Fill me in."

CHAPTER TWO

THE WOMAN was tall, quietly dressed and a young forty-odd. Her eyes were serene and guileless as she said: "You must be curious as to how I know about your case. It's quite simple—and unethical. We have a tipster in the clinic you visited. May I sit down?"

Dr. Oliver started and waved her to the dun-colored chair. A reaction was setting in. It was a racket—a cold-blooded racket preying on weak-minded victims silly with terror. "What's your proposition?" he asked, impatient to get it over with. "How much do I pay?"

"Nothing," the woman said calmly. "We usually pay poorer patients a little something to make up for the time they lose from work, but I presume you have a nest-egg. All this will cost you is a pledge of secrecy—and a little time."

"Very well," said Oliver stiffly. He had been hooked often enough by salesmen on no-money-down, free-trial-for-thirty-days, demonstration-for-consumer-reaction-only deals. He was on his guard.

"I find it's best to begin at the beginning," the woman said. "I'm an investment counselor. For the past five years I've also been a field representative for something called the Moorhead Foundation. The Moorhead Foundation was organized in 1915 by Oscar Moorhead, the patent-medicine millionaire. He died very deeply embittered by the attacks of the muckrakers; they called him a baby-poisoner and a number of other things. He always claimed that his preparations did just as much good as a visit to an average doctor of the period. Considering the state of medical education and licensing, maybe he was right.

"His will provided for a secret search for the cure of cancer. He must have got a lot of consolation daydreaming about it. One day the Foundation would announce to a startled world that it had cracked the problem and that old Oscar Moorhead was a servant of humanity and not a baby-poisoner after all.

"Maybe secrecy is good for research. I'm told that we know a number of things about neoplasms that the pathologists haven't hit on yet, including how to cure most types by radiation. My job, besides clipping coupons and reinvesting funds for the Foundation, is to find and send on certain specified types of cancer patients. The latest is what they call a Rotino 707-G. You. The technical people will cure you without surgery in return for a buttoned lip and the chance to study you for about a week. Is it a deal?"

Hope and anguish struggled in Dr. Oliver. *Could* anybody invent such a story? *Was* he saved from the horror of the knife?

"Of course," he said, his guts contracting, "I'll be expected to pay a share of the expenses, won't I? In common fairness?"

The woman smiled. "You think it's a racket, don't you? Well, it isn't. You don't pay a cent. Come with your pockets empty and leave your checkbook at home if you like. The Foundation gives you free room and board. I personally don't know the ins and outs of the

Foundation, but I have professional standing of my own and I assure you I'm not acting as a transmission belt to a criminal gang. I've *seen* the patients, Dr. Oliver. I send them on sick and I see them a week or so later completely well. It's like a miracle."

Dr. Oliver went distractedly to his telephone stand, picked up the red book and leafed through it.

"Roosevelt 4-19803," the woman said with amusement in her voice.

Doggedly he continued to turn the "W" pages. He found her. "Mgrt WINSTON. Invstmnt cnslr R04-19803." He punched the number.

"Winston investments," came the answer.

"Is Miss Winston there?" he asked.

"No, sir. She should be back by three if you wish to call again. May I take a message?"

"No message. But—would you describe Miss Winston for me?"

The voice giggled. "Why not? She's about five-eight, weighs about 135, brown hair and eyes and when last seen was wearing a tailored navy culotte suit with white cuffs and collar. What're you up to, mister?"

"Not a thing," he said. "Thanks." He hung up.

"Look," the woman said. She was emptying her wallet. "Membership card in the Investment Counselors' Guild. U.M.T. honorable discharge, even if it is a reduced photostat. City license to do business. Airline credit card. Residential rental permit. Business rental permit. City motor vehicle-parking permit. Blood-donor card."

He turned them over in his hands. The plastic-laminated things were unanswerable, and he gave himself up to relief and exultation. "I'm in, Miss Winston," he said in a fervent tone. "You should have seen the fellow they showed me after an operation like mine." He shuddered as he remembered Jimmy and his "splendid adjustment."

"I don't have to," the woman said, putting her wallet neatly away. "I saw my mother die. It was from one of the types of cancer they haven't licked yet. I get the usual commission on funds I handle for them, but I have a little personal interest in promoting the research end…"

"Oh. I see."

Suddenly she was brisk. "Now, Dr. Oliver, you've got to write whatever letters are necessary to explain that you're taking a little unplanned trip to think things out, or whatever it is you care to say. And pack enough personal items for at least a week. You can be on the jet in an hour if you're a quick packer and a quick letter-writer."

"Jet to where?" he asked, without thinking.

She smiled and shook her head.

Dr. Oliver shrugged and went to his typewriter. This was one gift horse he would not look in the mouth. Not after Jimmy.

Two hours later the fat sophomore Gillespie arrived full of lies and explanations with his overdue theme on the varous Elizabethan dramatists, which was full of borrowings and evasions. On Dr. Oliver's door there was pinned a small note in the doctor's handwriting that said: *Dr. Oliver will be away for several days for reasons of health.*

Gillespie scratched his head and shrugged. It was all right with him; Dr. Oliver was practically impossible to get along with, in spite of his vague reputation for brilliance. A schizoid, his girl called him. She majored in Psych.

CHAPTER THREE

THE MOORHEAD FOUNDATION proved to be in Mexico, in a remote valley of the state of Sonora. A jetliner took Dr. Oliver and Miss Winston most of the way very fast. Buses and finally an obsolete gasoline-powered truck driven by a Mexican took them the rest of the way very slowly. The buildings were a remodeled *rancheria* enclosed by a low, thick adobe wall.

Dr. Oliver, at the door of his comfortable bedroom, said: "Look, will I be treated immediately?" He seemed to have been asking that question for two days, but never to have got a plain yes or no answer.

"It all depends," Miss Winston said. "Your type of growth is definitely curable and they'll definitely cure it. But there may be a slight holdup while they're studying it. That's your part of the bargain, after all. Now I'll be on my way. I expect you're sleepy, and the lab people will take over from here. It's been a great pleasure."

They shook hands and Dr. Oliver had trouble suppressing a yawn. He was very sleepy, but he tried to tell Miss Winston how grateful he was. She smiled deprecatingly, almost cynically, and said: "We're using you too, remember? Well, goodbye."

Dr. Oliver barely made it to his bed.

His nightmares were terrible. There was a flashing light, a ringing bell and a wobbling pendulum that killed him, killed him, killed him, inch by inch, burying him under a mountain of flashes and clangs and blows while he was somehow too drugged to fight his way out.

HE REACHED fuzzily in the morning for the Dialit, which wasn't there. Good God! he marveled. Was one expected to get *up* for breakfast? But he found a button that brought a grinning Mexican with a breakfast tray. After he dressed, the boy took him to *los medicos*.

The laboratory, far down a deserted corridor, was staffed by two men and a woman. "Dr. Oliver," the woman said briskly. "Sit there." It was a thing like a dentist's chair with a suggestion of something ugly and archaic in a cup-shaped headrest.

Oliver sat, uneasily.

"The carcinoma," one of the men said to the other.

"Oh yes." The other man, quite ignoring Oliver as a person, wheeled over a bulky thing not much different in his eyes from a television camera. He pointed it at Oliver's throat and played it noiselessly over his skin. "That should do it," he said to the first man.

Oliver asked incredulously: "You mean I'm cured?" And he started to rise.

"Silence!" the woman snarled, rapping a button. Dr. Oliver collapsed back into the chair with a moan. Something had happened to him; something terrible and unimaginable. For a hideous split-second he had known undiluted pain, pure and uniform over every part of his body, interpreted variously by each. Blazing headache, eye-ache and earache, wrenching nausea, an agony of itching, colonic convulsions, stabbing ache in each of his bones and joints.

"But—" he began piteously.

"*Silence!*" the woman snarled, and rapped the button again.

He did not speak a third time but watched them with sick fear, cringing into the chair.

They spoke quite impersonally before him, lapsing occasionally into an unfamiliar word or so.

"Not more than twenty-seven *vistch,* I should say. Cardiac."

"Under a good—master, would you call it?—who can pace him, more."

"Perhaps. At any rate, he will not be difficult. See his record."

"Stimulate him again."

Again there was the split-second of hell on earth. The woman was studying a small sphere in which colors played prettily. "A good surge," she said, "but not a good recovery. What is the order?"

One of the men ran his finger over a sheet of paper—but he was looking at the woman. "Three military."

"What kind of military, *sobr'*?"

The man hastily rechecked the sheet with his index finger. "All for *igr' i khom.* I do not know what you would call it. A smallship? A killship?"

The other man said scornfully: "Either a light cruiser or a heavy destroyer."

"According to functional analogy I would call it a heavy destroyer," the woman said decisively. "A good surge is important to *igr' i khom.* We shall call down the destroyer to take on this Oliver and the two Stosses. Have it done."

"Get up," one of the men said to Oliver.

He got up. Under the impression that he could be punished only in the chair he said: "What—?"

"*Silence!*" the woman snarled, and rapped the button. He was doubled up with the wave of pain. When he recovered, the man took his arm and led him from the laboratory. He did not speak as he was half-dragged through endless corridors and shoved at last through a door into a large, sunlit room. Perhaps a dozen people were sitting about and turned to look.

He cringed as a tall, black-haired man said to him: "Did you just get out of the chair?"

"It's all right," somebody else said. "You can talk. We aren't—them. We're in the same boat as you. What's the story—heart disease? Cancer?"

"Cancer," he said, swallowing. "They had promised me—"

"They come through on it," the tall man said. "They do come through on the cures. Me, I have nothing to show for it. I was supposed to survey for minerals here—my name's Brockhaus. And this is Johnny White from Los Angeles. He was epileptic—bad seizures every day. But not any more. And this—but never mind. You can meet the rest later. You better sit down. How many times did they give it to you?"

"Four times," Dr. Oliver said. "What's all this about? Am I going crazy?"

The tall man forced him gently into a chair. "Take it easy," he said. "We don't know what it's all about."

"Damn it," somebody said, "the hell we don't. It's the commies, as plain as the nose on your face. Why else should they kidnap an experienced paper salesman like me?"

Brockhaus drowned him out: "Well, maybe it's the reds, though I doubt it. All we *know* is that they get us here, stick us in the chair and then take us away. And the ones they take away don't come back."

"They said something about cruisers and destroyers," Oliver mumbled. "And surges."

"You mean," Brockhaus said, "you stayed conscious all the way through?"

"Yes. Didn't you?"

"No, my friend. Neither did any of us. What are you, a United States Marine?"

"I'm an English professor. Oliver, of Columbia University."

Johnny White from Los Angeles threw up his hands. "He's an English professor," he yelled to the room. There was a cackle of laughter.

Oliver flushed, and White said hastily: "No offense, prof. But naturally we've been trying to figure out what—they—are after. Here we've got a poetess, a preacher, two lawyers, a salesman, a pitchman, a mining engineer, a dentist—and now an English professor."

"I don't know," Oliver mumbled. "But they did say something about cruisers and destroyers and surges."

Brockhaus was looking skeptical. "I didn't imagine it," Oliver said stubbornly. "And they said something about two Stosses."

"I guess you didn't imagine it," the tall man said slowly. "Two Stosses we've got. Ginny! This man heard something about you and your old man."

A WHITE-HAIRED MAN, stocky in build and with the big mobile face of an actor, thrust himself past

Brockhaus to confront Oliver. "What did they say?" he demanded.

A tired-looking blonde girl said to him: "Take it easy, Mike. The man's beat."

"It's all right," Oliver said to her. "They talked about an order. One of the men seemed to be reading something in Braille—but he didn't seem to have anything wrong with his eyes. And the woman said they'd call down the destroyer to take on me and the two Stosses. But don't ask me what it means."

"We've been here a week," the girl said. "They tell me that's as long as anybody stays."

"Young man," Stoss said confidentially, "since we're thrown together in this informal fashion I wonder if I could ask whether you're a sporting man? The deadly dullness of this place—" He was rattling a pair of dice casually.

"*Please,* Mike!" the girl said in a voice near hysteria. "Leave the man alone. What good's money here?"

"I'm a sporting man, Ginny," he said mildly. "A friendly game of chance to break the monotony—"

"You're a crook on wheels," the girl said bitterly, "and the lousiest monte operator that ever hit the road."

"My own daughter," the man said miserably. "My own daughter that got me into this lousy can—"

"How was I supposed to know it was a fake?" she flared. "And if you do die you won't die a junkie, by heavens!"

Oliver shook his head dazedly at their bickering.

"What will this young man think?" asked Stoss, with a try at laughing it off. "I can, see he's a person of indomitable will behind his mild exterior, a person who won't let the chance word of a malicious girl keep him from indulging in a friendly—"

"Yeah! I might believe that if I hadn't been hearing you give that line to farmhands and truck-drivers since I was seven. Now you're a cold-reader. My aching torso."

"Well," Stoss said with dignity, *"this* time, I happened to have meant it."

Oliver's head was throbbing. An indomitable will behind a mild exterior. It rang a bell somewhere deep inside him—a bell that clanged louder and louder until he felt his very body dissolve under its impact.

He dismissed the bizarre fantasy. He was Dr. Oliver of Columbia. He was Dr. Oliver of Columbia. He had always been.

The Stosses had drifted to a window, still quarreling. Brockhaus said after a pause: "It's a funny thing. He was on heroin. You should see his arms. When he first got here he went around begging and yelling for a fix of dope because he *expected* that he'd want it. But after a few hours he realized that he didn't want it at all. For the first time in twelve years, he says. Maybe it was the shocks in the chair. Maybe they did it intentionally. I don't know. The girl—there's nothing wrong with her. She just, came along to keep the old man company while he took the marvelous free cure."

A slight brunette woman with bangs was saying to him shyly: "Professor, I'm Mitty Worth. You may have heard of me—or not. I've had some pieces in the *New New Review.*"

"Delighted," Dr. Oliver said. "How did they get *you?*"

Her mouth twisted. "I was doing the Michoacán ruins. There was a man—a very handsome man—who persuaded me that he had made an archaeological find, that it would take the pen of a poet to do it justice—" She shrugged. "What's your field, professor?"

"Jacobean prose writers."

Her face lit up. "Thank God for somebody to talk to. I'm especially interested in Tom Fuller myself. I have a theory, you know, about the *Worthies of England*. Everybody automatically says it's a grab bag, you know, of everybody who happened to interest Fuller. But I think I can detect a definite *structure* in the book—"

Dr. Oliver of Columbia groped wildly in his memory. What was the woman running on about?

"I'm afraid I'm not familiar with the work," he said.

Mitty Worth was stunned.

"Or perhaps," Oliver said hastily, "I'm still groggy from the—the laboratory. Yes, I think that must be it."

"Oh," Mitty Worth said, and retreated.

Oliver sat and puzzled. Of course his specialty was the Jacobean prose writers. The foolish woman had made a mistake. Tom Fuller must be in another period. The *real* writers of Jacobean prose were—

Were—?

Dr. Oliver of Columbia, whose field was the Jacobean prose writers, didn't know any of them by name.

I'm going crazy, he decided wildly. I'm Oliver of Columbia. I wrote my thesis on—

What?

THE OLD FAKER was quite right. He was an indomitable will behind a seemingly mild exterior, and a ringing bell had something to do with it, and so did a flashing light and a wobbling pendulum, and so did

Marty Braun who could keep a tin can bouncing ten yards ahead of him as he walked firing from the hip, but Marty had a pair of star-gauge .44's and he wasn't a gun nut himself even if he could nip the ten-ring four out of five—

The world of Dr. Oliver was dissolving into delirium when his name was sharply called.

Everybody was looking at him as if he were something to be shunned, something with a curse laid on it. One of—them—was standing in the door. Dr. Oliver remembered what they could do. He got up hastily and hastily went through an aisle that cleared for him to the door as if by magic.

"Stand there," the man said to him. "The two Stoss people," he called. The old man and his daughter silently joined him.

"You must walk ahead of me," said the man.

They walked down the corridor and turned left at a command, and went through a handsome oak door into the sunlight. Gleaming in the sunlight was a vast disk-shaped thing.

Dr. Oliver of Columbia smiled quite suddenly and involuntarily. He knew now who he was and what was his mission.

He was Special Agent Charles Barker of Federal Security and Intelligence. He was in disguise—the most thorough disguise ever effected. His own personality had been obliterated by an unbroken month of narco-hypnosis, and for another unbroken month a substitute personality, that of the ineffectual Dr. Oliver, had been shoved into his head by every mechanical and psychological device that the F. S. I. commanded.

Twenty-four hours a day, waking and sleeping, records had droned in his ears and films had unreeled before his glazed drugged eyes, all pointing toward this moment of post-hypnotic revelation.

People vanished. People had always vanished. Blind Homer had undoubtedly heard many vague rumors and then incorporated them in his current repertory of songs about the recent war against the Trojans: vague rumors about a one-eyed thing that kidnapped men—to eat, of course.

People continued to vanish through the Roman Empire, the Middle Ages, the Renaissance and after, the growth of population and the invention of census machines. When the census machines were perfected everything was known statistically about everybody, though without invasion of privacy, for the machines dealt in percentages and not personalities. Population loss could be accounted for; such and such a percentage died, and this percentage pigged it drunkenly in Riveredge, and that percentage deserted wife and kids for a while before it was inevitably, automatically traced—

And there was a percentage left over. People still vanished.

The F. S. I. noted that three cancer patients in Morningside Heights, New York, had vanished last year, so they had decided to give (Temporary) Special Agent Charles Barker a cancer by nagging a harmless throat polyp with dyes and irritants, and installed him in Morningside Heights to vanish—and do something about it.

The man marched the two Stosses and Barker-Oliver into the spaceship.

Minutes later a smashing takeoff acceleration dashed them unconscious to the deck.

CHAPTER FOUR

IN AN EARTHLY NAVY they would have called Gori "Guns" in the wardroom. He didn't look like an officer and a gentleman, or a human being for that matter, and the batteries of primary and secondary weapons he ruled over did not look like cannon. But Gori had a pride and a class feeling that would have made familiar sense in any navy. He voiced it in his needling of Lakhrut: a brother officer but no fighting man; a sweat-soaked ruler of the Propulsion Division whose station was between decks, screwing the last flicker of drive from the units.

Languidly Gori let his fingertips drift over a page of text; he was taking a familiarization course in propulsion. "I don't understand," he said to Lakhrut, "why one shouldn't treat the units with a little more formality. My gun-pointers, for example—"

Lakhrut knew he was being needled, but had to pretend otherwise. Gori was somewhat his senior. "Gun-pointers are one thing," he said evenly. "Propulsion units are another. I presume you've worked the globes."

Gori raised his fingers from the page in surprise. "Evidently you—people between decks don't follow the Games," he said. "I have a Smooth Award from the last meet but one."

"What class vessel?"

"Single-seater. And a beauty! Built to my orders, stripped to a bare hull microns in thickness."

"Then you know working the globes isn't easy. But—with all respect—I don't believe you know that working a globe under orders, shift after shift, with no stake in the job and no hope or relief ever is most infernally heartbreaking. You competed for the Smooth Award and won it and slept for a week, I dare say, and are still proud—don't misunderstand me: *rightly* proud—of the effort. But the propulsion units aren't competing for anything. They've been snatched away from their families—I'm not certain; I believe a family system prevails—and they *don't* like it. We must break them of that. Come and see the new units."

Gori reluctantly followed Lakhrut to the inport where unconscious figures were being stacked.

"Pah! They stink!" he said.

"A matter of diet. It goes away after they've been on our rations for a while."

Gori felt one of the figures curiously. "Clothes," he said in surprise. "I thought—"

Lakhrut told him wearily: "They have been wearing clothes for quite a while now. Some five thousand of their years." That had been a dig too. Gori had been reminding him that he was not greatly concerned with the obscure beasts between decks; that he, Lakhrut, must clutter his mind with such trivial details while Gori was splendidly free to man his guns if there should be need. "I'll go and see my driver," he snapped.

When he left, Gori sat down and laughed silently.

Lakhrut went between decks to the banks of units and swiftly scanned them. Number Seven was sleeping, with deep lines of fatigue engraved on his mind. He would be the next to go; indeed he should have been shot through the spacelock with Three, Eight-Female and Twelve. At the first opportunity— His driver approached.

"Baldwin," he snapped at the driver, "will you be able to speak with the new units?"

Baldwin, a giant who had been a mere propulsion unit six months ago and was fiercely determined never to be one again, said in his broken speech: "Believe it. Will make to understand somewise. They may not— converse—my language called English. Will make to understand somewise."

BARKER AWOKE staring into dull-red lights that looked unbelievably like old-fashioned incandescent lamps. Beside him a girl was moaning with shock and fear. In the dull light he could make out her features: Ginny Stoss. Her father was lying unconscious with his head in her lap.

A brutal hand yanked him to his feet—there was gravity! But there was no time to marvel over it. A burly giant in a gray kilt was growling at him: "You speak English?"

"Yes. What's all this about? Where are we?"

He was ignored. The giant yanked Ginny Stoss to her feet and slapped her father into consciousness as the girl winced and Barker balled his fists helplessly. The giant said to the three of them:

"My name's Baldwin. You call me mister. Come on."

He led them, the terrified girl, the dazed old man and the rage-choked agent through spot-polished metal corridors to—

A *barbershop*, Barker thought wildly. Rows and rows of big adjustable chairs gleaming dully under the red lights, people sitting in them, at least a hundred people. And then you saw there was something archaic and ugly about the cup-shaped head rests fitted to the chairs. And then you saw that the people, men and women, were dirty, unkempt and hopeless-eyed, dressed in rags or nothing at all.

Ginny Stoss screamed sharply when she saw Lakhrut. He was not a pretty sight with his single bulging orb above the nose. It pointed at her and Lakhrut spat guttural syllables at Baldwin. The burly giant replied, cringing and stammering. The monster's orb aimed at Barker, and he felt a crawling on the surface of his brain—as if fingers were trying to grasp it.

Barker knew what to do; more important, he did it. He turned off Barker. He turned on Dr. Oliver, the erudite scared rabbit.

Lakhrut scanned them suspiciously. The female was radiating sheer terror; good. The older male was frightened too, but his sense of a reality was clouded; he detected a faint undertone of humor. *That* would go. The younger man—Lakhrut stooped forward in a reflex associated with the sense of smell. The younger man— men?—no; man—the younger man—

Lakhrut stopped trying to scan him. He seemed to be radiating on two bands simultaneously, which was not possible, Lakhrut decided that he wasn't focusing properly, that somebody else's radiation was leaking and that the younger man's radiation was acting as a carrier wave for it. And felt vaguely alarmed and ashamed of himself. He ought to be a better scanner than he was.

"Baldwin," he said, "question that one closely."

The hulking driver asked: "You want name?"

"Of course not, fool! Question him about anything. I want to scan his responses."

Baldwin spoke to the fellow unintelligibly and the fellow replied unintelligibly. Lakhrut almost smiled with relief as the questioning progressed. The odd double-band effect was vanishing and the young man radiated simple fright.

Baldwin said laboriously: "Says is teacher of language and—tales of art. Says where is this and why have—"

"That's enough," he told the driver. "Install them." None of this group was dangerous enough to need killing.

SIT THERE," Baldwin told Barker, jerking his thumb at an empty chair.

Barker felt the crawling fingers withdraw, and stifled a thought of triumph. They *had* him, this renegade and his cyclops boss. They had him like a bug underfoot to be squashed at a whim, but there had been some kind of test and he had bluffed them. Wearing the persona of Oliver, he quavered: "What *is* this terrible place, Mr. Baldwin? *Why* should I sit there?"

Baldwin moved in with a practiced ring shuffle and swung his open palm against the side of Barker's head. The agent cried out and nursed the burning cheek. Baldwin would never know how close he came that moment to a broken back...

He collapsed limply into the chair and felt it mould to him almost like a living thing. Plates slid under his thighs and behind his shoulder blades, accommodating themselves to his body.

"Just to show you nobody's fooling," Baldwin said grimly. He pressed a button on the chair and again something indescribably painful happened, wringing his bones and muscles to jelly for a timeless instant of torment. He did not faint; it was there and gone too quickly for the vascular system to make such an adjustment. He slumped in the chair, gasping.

Baldwin said: "Take hold of the two handles." He was surprised to find that he could move. He took hold of two spherical handles. They were cold and slimy— dry. Baldwin said: "You have to make the handles turn rough, like abrasive paper. You do it different ways. I can't tell you how. Everybody has a different way. Some people just concentrate on the handles. Other people just try to make their minds a blank and that works for them. You just find your own way and do it when we tell you to. Or you get the pain again. That's all."

Barker heard him move down the line and repeat the speech in substantially the same words to the Stosses.

Baldwin was no puzzle. He was just a turncoat bastard. The wrecked, ragged men and women with lackluster eyes sitting around him were no puzzle. Not after the pain. Baldwin's boss, the cyclops—

How long had this been going on? Since Homer?

He bore down on the spherical handles. Amazingly they went from silk-smooth to paper-coarse and then to sandstone-gritty. Baldwin was back, peering to look at an indicator of some unimaginable kind. "That's very good," the big man said. "You keep that up and some day you'll get out of the chair like me."

Not like you, you bastard. Not like you. He choked down the thought. If the boss were here it would have undone him.

There were mechanical squeals and buzzers. Those who were sleeping in their chairs awoke instantly, with panic on their faces, visible even in the dim red light.

"All right," Baldwin was shouting. *"Give,* you bastards! Five seconds and we cut you in. *Give,* Morgan, or it's the Pain! Silver, make it move! I ain't forgetting anything, Silver—next time it's three jolts. Give, you bastards! *Give!"*

Barker gave in a frenzy of concentration. Under his sweaty palms the globes became abrasive. In five seconds there was a thudding shock through his body that left him limp. The globes went smooth and Baldwin was standing over him: "Make it go, Oliver, or it's the Pain. Make it go."

Somehow, he did.

It seemed to go on for hours while the world rocked and reeled about him, whether subjectively or objectively he could not tell. And at last there was the roar: "Let it go now. Everybody off."

Racking vibration ceased and he let his head nod forward limply.

From the chair in front of him came an exhausted whisper: "He's gone now. Someday I'm going to—"

"Can we talk?" Barker asked weakly.

"Talk, sing, anything you want."

There was a muttering and stirring through the big room. From the chair in front, hopefully: "Do you happen to be from Rupp City? My family—"

"No," Barker said. "I'm sorry. What is all this? What are we doing?"

The exhausted whisper said: "All this is an armed merchantman of the A'rkhov-Yar. We're running it. We're galley slaves."

CHAPTER FIVE

THREE FEEDINGS LATER the man from Rupp City leaped from his chair, howling, and threw himself on a tangle of machinery in the center aisle. He was instantly electrocuted.

Before he died he had told Barker in rambling, formless conversations that he had it figured out; the star-people simply knew how to amplify psychokinetic energy. He thought he could trace eighteen stages of amplification through the drive machinery.

The death was a welcome break in the monotony. Barker was horrified to discover that was his principal reaction to it, but he was not alone.

They were fed water and moist yellow cakes that tasted like spoiled pork. Normally they worked three shifts in rotation. Only now and then were they all summoned for a terrific surge; usually they had only to keep steerage way on the vessel. But eight hours spent bearing down on the spherical handles, concentrating, was an endless agony of boredom and effort. If your attention wandered, you got the Pain. Barker got it five times in fifteen feedings. Others got it ten or twelve. Ginny Stoss was flighty of mind; she got it twenty times, and after that, never. She mumbled continuously after that and spent all her time in practice, fingering the handles and peering into the bad light with dim, monomaniac eyes.

There was an efficient four-holer latrine, used without regard to sex or privacy. Sex was a zero in their lives, despite the mingling of men and women. When they slept in their chairs, they slept. The Pain and then death were the penalties for mating, and also their energy was low. The men were not handsome and the women were not beautiful. Hair and beards grew and straggled—why not? Their masters ignored them as far as clothing went. If the things they wore when they came aboard fell apart, very well, they fell apart. They weren't going any place.

It was approximately eight hours working the globular handles, eight hours sleeping, and eight hours spent in rambling talk about the past, with many lies told of riches and fame. Nobody ever challenged a lie; why should they?

Bull-necked Mr. Baldwin appeared for feedings, but he did not eat with them. The feedings were shift-change time, and he spent them in harangues and threats.

Barker sucked up to Baldwin disgustingly, earning the hatred of all the other "units." But they knew next to nothing, and what he desperately needed was information. All they knew was that they had been taken aboard—a year ago? Six years ago? A month ago? They could only guess. It was impossible to keep track of time within the changeless walls of the room. Some of them had been taken directly aboard. Some had been conveyed in a large craft with many others and then put aboard. Some had served in other vessels, with propulsion rooms that were larger or smaller, and then put aboard. They had been told at one time or another that they were in the A'rkhov-Yar fleet, and disputed feebly about the meaning and pronunciation. It was more of a rumor than a fact.

Barker picked a thread from his tie each day to mark the days, and sucked up to Baldwin.

Baldwin liked to be liked, and pitied himself. "You think," he asked plaintively, "I'm inhuman? You think I want to drive the units like I do? I'm as friendly as the next guy, but it's dog eat dog, isn't it? If I wasn't driving I'd be in a chair getting driven, wouldn't I?"

"I can see that, Mr. Baldwin. And it takes character to be a leader like you are."

"You're damned right it does. And if the truth was known, I'm the best friend you people have. If it wasn't me it'd be somebody else who'd be worse. Lakhrut said to me once that I'm too easy on the units and I stood right up to him and said there wasn't any sense to wearing them out and not having any drive when the going gets hot."

"I think it's amazing, Mr. Baldwin, the way you picked up the language. That takes *brains*."

Baldwin beamed modestly. "Oh, it ain't too hard. For instance—"

INSTRUCTION BEGAN. It was not too hard, because Baldwin's vocabulary consisted of perhaps four hundred words, all severely restricted to his duties. The language was uninflected; it could have been an old and stable speech. The grammar was merely the word-order of logic: subject, verb, object. Outstandingly, it was a guttural speech. There were remnants of "tonality" in it. Apparently it had once been a sung language like Chinese, but had evolved even out of that characteristic.

Phonemes that once had been low-toned were now sounded back in the throat; formerly high-toned phonemes were now forward in the throat. That sort of thing he had picked up from "Oliver."

Barker hinted delicately at it, and Baldwin slammed a figurative door in his face. "I don't know," he growled. "I don't go asking smart questions. You better not either."

Four more threads were snapped from the fringe of Barker's tie before Baldwin came back, hungry for flattery. Barker was on shift, his head aching with the pointless, endless, unspeakably dull act of concentration when the big man shook his shoulder and growled: "You can layoff. Seven, eight—it don't matter. The others can work harder."

He slobbered thanks.

"Ah, that's all right. I got a good side to me too, see? I said to Lakhrut once—"

And so on, while the other units glared.

"Mr. Baldwin, this word *khesor,* does it mean the whole propulsion set-up or the energy that makes it work? You say, *'Lekhrut a'g khesor-takh'* for 'Lakhrut is the boss of propulsion,' right?"

Baldwin's contempt was kindly. "For a smart man you can ask some damned stupid questions. What difference does it make?" He turned to inspect the globes for a moment and snarl at Ginny Stoss: "What's the matter with you? You want the Pain again? *Give!*"

Her lips moved in her endless mutter and her globe flared bright.

The bull-necked man said confidingly: "Of course I wouldn't really give her the Pain again. But you have to scare them a little from time to time."

"Of course, Mr. Baldwin. You certainly know psychology." *One of these days I'm going to murder you, you bastard.*

"Sure; it's the only way. Now, you know what *ga'lt* means?"

"No, Mr. Baldwin."

The bull-necked pusher was triumphant. "There is no word for it in English. It's something they can do and we can't. They can look right into your head if they want to. *'Lakhrut ga'lt takh-lyur-Baldwin'* means 'Lakhrut looks right into Underchief Baldwin's head and reads his mind."

"Do they do it all the time?"

"No. I think it's something they learn. I don't think all of them can do it either—or maybe not all of them learn to do it. I got a theory that Lakhrut's a *ga'lt* specialist."

"Why, Mr. Baldwin?"

Baldwin grinned. "To screen out troublemakers. No hard feelings, Oliver, but do you notice what a gutless bunch of people you got here? Not a rebel in a carload. Chicken-livered. Don't take it personal—either you got it or you don't."

"But *you,* Mr. Baldwin why didn't the screening stop you?"

"I got a theory about that. I figure he let me through on purpose because they needed a hard guy to do just what I'm doing. After I got broke in on the globes it wasn't hardly any time at all before I got to be *takh-lyur.*"

You're wrong, you bastard. You're the yellowest coward aboard.

"That must be it, Mr. Baldwin. They know a leader when they see one."

FOUR THREADS LATER he knew that he had acquired all of the language Baldwin had to give him. During his sleep period he went to old Stoss' chair. Stoss was on rest. He was saying vaguely to a gray-haired woman in the chair in front of his: "Boston, Atlanta, Kansas City—all the prominent cities of the nation, my dear lady. I went in with a deck of cards and came out of each with a diamond ring and a wallet filled with winnings. My hands were sure, my voice was friendly—"

"Atlanta," the woman sighed. "The Mathematics Teachers Association met there in '87, or was it '88? I remember gardens with old brick walls—or was that Charleston? Yes, I think it was Charleston."

"—In one memorable session of stud behind locked doors in the old Muehlbach Hotel I was high on the third card with the Jack of clubs and the ten of diamonds, with the ace of clubs for my hole-card. Well, madam—"

"—We had terrible trouble in the school one year with the boys and girls gambling in the reactor room, and worse if you can believe it. The reactor man was their 'look-out,' so to speak, so naturally we tried to have him discharged. But the union wouldn't let—"

"Well, madam, there was seven hundred-odd dollars in the pot—"

"Mr. Stoss," Barker said.

The old man studied him coolly for a moment, staring at him intently. Then he said: "You know I don't believe I care to talk to you, sir. There's just something about you that I…well…as I was saying, ma'am, there was—"

"I'm going to kill Baldwin," Barker told him.

He was instantly alert, and instantly scared. "But the danger," he whispered. "Won't they take it out on all of us? And he's a big brute—"

"So maybe he'll end up killing me. But I'm going to try. I want you to go to the latrine the next time Baldwin shows up. But don't quite go in. Stand and watch the corridor. If there's anybody coming, lift your hand. I'll only need a few seconds. Either way, it'll be finished by then."

"The danger," whispered Stoss. His eyes wandered about and then over to his daughter's chair. She was sound asleep. And her lips still moved lightly in her endless muttering. "All right," the old man said at last. "I'll help you."

"Can you imagine that?" the woman said, still amazed after all these years. "The man was caught *in flagrente delicto*, so to speak, and the union wouldn't let the principal discharge him without a full public hearing, and naturally the publicity would have been most distasteful so we were forced to—"

Barker padded back to his chair, a gaunt man in stinking rags, wild-haired and sporting a beard in which gray hairs were beginning to appear.

There had to be a lookout. Three times since takeoff Lakhrut had appeared in the doorway for a moment to stare at the units. Twice other people had actually come into the room with Baldwin to probe through the tangle of machinery down the center aisle with long, slender instruments.

It might have been one hour; it might have been three; it might have been seven. Baldwin appeared, followed by the little self-propelled cart. It began to make its rounds, stopping at each chair long enough for the bottle of water and the dish of soggy cake to be picked off. Stoss, looking perfectly innocent, passed Barker's chair.

Barker got up and went to the pusher. Stoss was looking through the door, and did not wave. The cart clicked and rolled to the next chair. "Something wrong, Oliver?" Baldwin asked.

"I'm going to kill you, you bastard."

"*What?*" Baldwin's mouth was wide open, but an instant later he dropped into a fighter's crouch instinctively.

His ankle hooked behind Baldwin's foot. The bull-necked man threw a sweeping punch, which Barker ducked. Baldwin then tried to clinch when Barker butted him in the chest. Baldwin went sprawling over into the tangle of machinery at the same spot where the man from Rupp City had fried. There were sparks and stench. Then it was over.

Baldwin's mouth was still open and his body contorted. Barker could imagine him saying: "You think I'm inhuman? You think I want to drive the units like I do?" And he could also imagine him roaring: "*Give,* damn you!"

Steadily Barker went back to his seat in time for the cart to click by. Stoss, his face at this point a perfect blank, padded back from the latrine. There was a murmur and stir that grew louder in the big rectangular room.

CHAPTER SIX

LAKHRUT was lying in his hammock in the dark, his fingers idly reading. It should have been a manual; instead it was an historical romance. His fingers skipped a half-page describing an old-style meal and slowed to absorb the description of the fight in which it ended.

"Yar raises his revolver charged with powder and ball. Who is so brave as Yar? He pulls back the trigger and presses the hammer of the death-dealing tube! The flash of flame shows the face of Lurg! But smoke from the tube obscures—"

His fingers jerked from the page as the commander's voice roared through his cubicle: *"Lakhrut!* Look to your units! We have no steerage way!"

He leaped from the hammock and raced through the vessel cursing Baldwin, the maintenance crew, the units and every soul on board.

He took in the situation at a glance. Baldwin lying spread-eagled and charred against the conversion grids. The units yammering and terrified in their chairs, none of them driving. Into a wall mike he snapped to the bridge: "My driver's dead, Commander. He got a charge from the conversion grids—"

"Stop your gabbing and give me power, you fool!"

Deathly pale, Lakhrut turned to the disorganized units and tried to talk to them in remembered scraps of English. (He should have worked more with his driver on it.

He should have worked more.) They only gawked at him, and he swore in A'rkhov—

But one of the units was doing something that made sense. He was yelling in English, pointing to the chairs. And a dozen of the units resumed their places and began to drive, feebly at first and then better.

That was taken care of. He turned to the machinery and checked rapidly through the stages of amplification. They were clear; the commander, curse him, was getting his power. The fellow who had yelled at the units was standing by him when the inspection was completed. Startlingly, he said in A'rkhov, though with a fearsome accent: "Can I serve Lakhrut-*takh?*"

With considerable effort, Lakhrut scanned him. Obedience, fear, respect, compliance. All was well. He asked him coldly: "Who are you that you should speak the tongue?"

"Name is Oliver. I studied languages. Baldwin-*takh-lyur* taught me the tongue." Lakhrut scanned; it all was true.

"How did he die?"

"I did not see. Oliver was not looking. I was in darkness."

Asleep, was he trying clumsily to say? Lakhrut scanned. There was no memory of the death-scene in the scared, compliant mind of this unit. But something nagged Lakhrut and teased at his mind. "Did you kill him?" he snapped.

The flood of horror and weakness he scanned was indubitable. The unit babbled brokenly: "No, Lakhrut-*takh!* No! I could not kill! I could not kill!" Well, *that* was true enough. It had been a silly thing to ask.

"Take me," Lakhrut said, "to each unit in turn and ask them whether they killed the *takh-lyur.*"

This Oliver did, and reported twenty-two denials while Lakhrut scanned each. Each was true; none of the twenty-two minds into which he peered was shuddering with the aftermath of murder; none seemed to have the killer's coldness and steel.

Lakhrut said to the wall mike: "Power is restored. I have established that my driver's death was accidental. I have selected a new driver from among the units," He turned off the mike after a curt acknowledgment and said to Oliver: "Did you understand? I meant you." At the mike again he called two maintenance men to clear the conversion grid and space the body.

"Establish unit shifts and then come with me," he told Oliver. He then waited for his new driver to instruct the gangs. He ceased scanning; his head was aching abominably.

BARKER felt the fingers leave his brain and breathed deeper. Dr. Oliver of Columbia, the whining incubus on him, was bad company. His own memory of the past few minutes was vague and fragmentary. In jittery terror Dr. Oliver had yelled at the units to man their chairs before they all were killed for disobedience. In abject compliance, Dr. Oliver had placed himself at Lakhrut's orders. And he had heard that he would be the new slave driver with almost tearful gratitude. To be shaved and clean again! To dine again! Barker wanted to spit. Instead he divided the units into new shifts and followed Lakhrut from the oblong room.

He washed and used a depilatory powder that burned horribly as the cyclops monster called Lakhrut silently watched. Somebody brought him shorts that fit. Apparently the concept of a uniform was missing—so even was style. He saw passing on the upper decks crew "men" in trousers, gowns, kilts and indescribable combinations of these. The only common note was simplicity and a queer, vulgar absence of dash, as if nobody cared what he looked like as long as the clothes didn't get in his way.

"That's enough," Lakhrut said, as Barker was trying to comb his wetted hair with his fingers. "Come with me."

Back between decks they went to a cubicle near the drive room—a combination of kitchen, cramped one-man office and hammock-space. Lakhrut briskly showed Barker how to draw and prepare the food for the units—it was the first time he suspected that Baldwin had cooked for them—and how to fill in a daily report on the condition of the units. It was hardly writing; he simply had to check a box in the appropriate column next to the unit's number. His "pen" flowed clear plastic, which bonded to the paper in a raised ridge. The "printed" form was embossed with raised lines. Barker could make nothing of the numerals that designated the units or the column-headings; the alphabet rang no bells in his memory or the Oliver-memory. But that would come later.

THE COMMANDER was winding up his critique, and his division officers were perspiring freely.

"As to the recent gun-drill, I have very little to say. What, gentlemen, *is* there to say about the state of training, the peak of perfection which enabled Gori-*takh's* crews to unlimber, train and dry-fire their primary and secondary batteries in a mere two hundred and thirty-six and eleven-twelfths *vistch?* I am sure the significance of this figure will be clear to us all when I point out that the average space engagement lasts one hundred and eighteen *vistch*. Is the significance clear to you, Gori-*takh?*"

"Yes, Commander," said the division officer, very pale.

"Perfectly clear?"

"Yes. Commander," Gori said, wishing he was dead.

"Good. Then we will go on to pleasanter subjects. Propulsion has been excellent and uninterrupted since our last meeting. Steerageway has been satisfactorily maintained, units are in reasonable health, mechanical equipment checks out between Satisfactory and Excellent. The surprise-drill calls for driving surges were responded to promptly and with vigor. Lakhrut-*takh,* you are to be commended."

He left the compartment on that note, and the division officers sprawled, sighed and gave other signs of release from tension.

Lakhrut said to Gori, with the proper blend of modesty and sympathetic blandness:

"It's just luck, you know. Your bad luck and my good luck. I happen to have stumbled on the most extraordinary driver in the fleet. The fellow is amazing. He speaks the tongue, he's pitiless to the units, and he's wild to anticipate my every wish. He's even trying to learn the mechanism."

A *takh* vaguely corresponding to the Paymaster of a British naval vessel, with a touch of Chaplain and Purser thrown in, said: "What's that? Isn't there a *Yongsong* order about that? Perhaps I'd better—"

Lakhrut hastily balanced the benefit of a lie at this point against the chance that the *takh,* a master-scanner because of his office, might scan him for veracity. Since scanning of equals was bad manners and he felt himself the *takh's* equal at least after the commander's sweet words of praise, he lied. " 'Trying' does not mean 'succeeding,' " he said, letting his voice sound a little hurt. "I'm surprised that you should think I'd let an Outworlder into our secrets. No, the man is merely cracking his brains over an obsolete manual or two of advanced theory. He can barely read, as I've repeatedly verified by scanning. His tactile-memory barely exists. What brutes these Outlanders are! I doubt that they can tell fur from marble."

The *takh* said: "That is extremely unlikely in view of their fairly-advanced mechanical culture. Take me to him; I shall scan him."

Gori tried not to look exultant as Lakhrut, crestfallen, led the *takh* from the room.

The *takh* was somehow alarmed when he saw Lakhrut's driver. Even before scanning he could see that the fellow was tough. Vague thoughts of a spotter from Fleet Command or a plant from some enemy—or nominally friendly—fleet drifted through his head before he could clamp down on them. He said to the driver: "Who are you and what was your occupation?" And simultaneously he scanned deep.

The driver said: "Name is Oliver, *takh*. Teacher of language and letters."

The personality-integral included: Inferiority. ? Self-deprecation/Neurosis. ? …Weakling's job/Shame. ? Traumata…

A light. A bell. A pendulum.

Fear. Fear.

Being buried, swallowed, engulfed.

The *takh* was relieved. There was no danger in such a personality-integral. But the matter of security—he handed the driver a fingering-piece, a charming abstraction by the great Kh'hora. It had cost him his pay for an entire tour of duty and it was quite worth it. Kh'hora had carved it at the height of his power, and his witty juxtapositions of textures were unsurpassed to this day. It could be fingered a dozen ways, each a brilliant variation on a classic theme.

The driver held it stupidly.

"Well?" demanded the *takh*, his brows drawing together. He scanned.

The driver said: "Please, *takh*, I don't know what to do with it."

The personality-integral included: Fear. Bewilderment. Ignorance. Blankness.

"Finger it, you fool!"

The driver fumbled at the piece and the *takh* scanned. The tactile impressions were unbelievably obtuse and blurry. There was no emotional response to them whatsoever except a faint, dull gratification at a smooth boss on the piece. And the imbecile kept *looking* at it.

It was something like sacrilege. The *takh* snatched the piece back indignantly. "Describe it," he said, controlling himself.

The fellow began to maunder about its visual appearance while the *takh* scanned. It was true; he had practically no tactile memory.

The *takh* left abruptly with Lakhrut. "You were right," he said. "If it amuses the fellow to pretend that he can read, I see no obstacle. And if it contributes to the efficiency of your department, we all shine that much brighter." (More literally, with fuller etymological values, his words could be rendered: "If it amuses the fellow to pretend that he fingers wisdom, my hands are not grated. And if it smoothes your quarry wall, we all hew more easily.")

Lakhrut's hands were not grated either; it was a triumphant vindication of his judgment.

And so, for departmental efficiency, he let his marvelous driver have all the books he wanted.

CHAPTER SEVEN

BARKER'S head ached and his eyes felt ready to fall out of their sockets. He did, not dare take rubbings of the books, which would have made them reasonably legible. He had to hold them slantwise to the light in his cubicle and read the shadows of the characters. Lakhrut had taken the time to teach him the Forty-Three Syllables, condescendingly, and the rest was up to him. He had made the most of it.

An imagery derived more from tactile than visual senseimpressions sometimes floored him with subtleties—as, he was sure, an intensely visual English nature poem would have floored Lakhrut. But he progressed.

Lakhrut had brought him a mish-mash of technical material and trashy novelettes and a lexicon. The *takh* who had made such a fuss about the chipped pebble had brought him something like a Bible. Pay dirt!

It seems that in the beginning, Spirit had created Man—which is what the A'rkhov-Yar called the A'arkhov-Yar—and set him to rule over all lesser creation. Man had had his ups and downs on the Planet, but Spirit had seen to it that he annihilated after sanguinary, millennium-long battles, his principal rivals for the Planet. These appeared to have been twelve-footed brutes who fought with flint knives in their first four feet.

And then Spirit had sent the Weak People to the Planet in a spaceship. Schooled to treachery in the long struggle against the knife-wielding beasts, Man had greeted the Weak People with smiles, food and homage. The Weak People had foolishly taught them the art of writing, had foolishly taught Man their sciences. And then the Weak People had been slain, all twelve of them, in an hour of blood.

Barker somehow saw the Weak People as very tired, very gentle, very guileless survivors of a planetary catastrophe beyond guessing. But the book didn't say.

So the A'rkhov-Yar stole things. Science. People. Let George do it, appeared to be their morality, and then steal it from George. Well, they'd had a hard upbringing fighting down the Knifers, which was no concern of his. They'd been man-stealing for lord knows how long; they'd made turncoats like the late Mister Baldwin, and judas goats like neat Miss Winston, disgusting creatures preying on their own kind.

From the varied reading matter he built up a sketchy picture of the A'rkhov-Yar universe. There were three neighboring stars with planetary systems, and the cyclops had swarmed over them once the guileless Weak People had shown them space flight. First they had driven their own ships with their own wills. Then they had learned that conquered races could be used equally well, so they had used them. Then they learned that conquered races tended to despair and die out.

"THEN," he said savagely to old man Stoss, "they showed the one flash of creative intelligence in their career—unless they stole it from one of their subjects.

They invaded Earth—secretly. Without knowing it, we're their slave-breeding pen. If we knew it, we'd either fight and win, or fight and lose—and die out in despair."

"The one flash?" Stoss asked dryly, looking about them at the massive machinery.

"Stolen. All stolen. They have nations, trades and wars—but this is a copy of the Weak People's ship; all their ships are. And their weapons are the meteor screens and sweepers of the Weak People. With stolen science they've been stealing people. I think at a rate of thousands per year. God knows how long it's been going on—probably since the Neolithic age. You want proof of their stupidity? The way they treat us. It leads to a high death rate and fast turnover. That's bad engineering, bad economics and bad housekeeping. Look at the lights they use—low-wattage incandescents! As inefficient lamps as were ever designed—"

"I've got a thought about those lights," Stoss said. "The other day when Lakhrut was inspecting and you were passing out the food I took two cakes instead of one—just to keep in practice. I used slight of hand, misdirection—but Lakhrut didn't misdirect worth a damn. He slapped the pain button and I put the extra cake back. What does it mean when the hand is quicker than the eye but the sucker isn't fooled?"

"I don't get you."

"What if those aren't very inefficient lamps but very efficient heaters?"

"They're blind," whispered Barker. "My God, you've got to be right! The lamps, the tactile culture, the embossed writing. And that thing that looks like an eye—it's their mind-reading organ, so it can't be an eye

after all. You can't perform two radically different functions with the same structure."

"It's worth thinking about," old man Stoss said.

"I could have thought about it for a million years without figuring that out, Stoss. How did you do it?"

The old man looked modest. "Practice. Long years of it. When you want to take a deacon for a long score on the con game, you study him for his weaknesses. You don't assume he hasn't got any just because he's a deacon, or a doctor, or a corporation treasurer. Maybe it's women, or liquor, or gambling, or greed.

You just play along, what interests him interests you, everything he says is wise and witty, and sooner or later he lets you know what's his soft spot. Then, lad, you've got him. You make his world revolve around his little weakness. You cater to it and play it up and by and by he gets to thinking that you're the greatest man in the world, next to him, and the only real friend he'll ever have. Then you 'tell the tale,' as we say. And the next sound you hear is the sweetest music this side of Heaven, the squealing of a trimmed sucker."

"You're a revolting old man," said Barker, "and I'm glad you're here."

"I'm glad you're here too," the old man said. And he added with a steady look: "Whoever you are."

"You might as well know. Charles Barker—F. S. I. agent. They fished me out of the Riveredge gutter because I may or may not have telepathic flashes, and they put me on the disappearance thing."

Stoss shook his head unhappily. "At my age, cooperating with the F. S. I., I'll never live it down."

Barker said: "They've got sound to go on, of course. They hear movements, air currents. They carry in their heads a sound picture—but it isn't a 'picture'; damn language!—of their environment. They can't have much range or discrimination with that sense; too much noise hashing up the picture. They're probably heat-detectors, too. If bedbugs and mosquitoes can use heat for information, so can these things. Man could do it too if he had to, but we have eyes. The heat-sense must be short range too; blackbody radiation falls off proportional to the fourth power of the distance. It's beginning to fit together. They don't go *very* near those incandescent bulbs ever, do they? They keep about a meter distant?"

"Yes, I've noticed that. Anything closer must be painful to the heat sense—'blinding,' you might say."

"Then that leaves their telepathy. That specialist came into this room to examine me, which tells us something about the range. Something—but not enough."

Stoss said: "A person might pretend to throw something at one of them from a distance of ten yards. If the creature didn't notice, we'd know they don't have a ten-yard range with sound, heat or telepathy. And the next day he could try it at nine yards. And so on, until it noticed."

"And blew the person in half with those side-arms they carry," said Barker. "Who volunteers for the assignment, Stoss?"

"Not I," the old man said hastily. "Let's be practical. But perhaps I could persuade Miss Trimble?"

"The math teacher? Hell, no. If things work out, we're going to need all the mathematical talent we've got."

They conferred quietly, deciding which of their fellow Earthmen would be persuaded to sacrifice himself. The choice fell on a nameless, half-mad youngster in the third seat of the second tier; he spoke to nobody and glared suspiciously over his food and drink.

"But can you do it?" asked Barker.

Stoss was offended. "In my time," he said, "I've taken some fifty-five really big scores from suckers. I've persuaded people who love money better than life itself to turn their money over to me, and I've sent them to the bank for more."

"Do your best," Barker said.

WHAT APPROACH the old swindler did use, he never learned. But the next day Third Seat, Second Tier, rose during the doling out of the food and pretended to hurl his plate at Lakhrut. The cyclops, ten meters away, stalked serenely on and the young man collapsed in an ecstasy of fright.

The next day it was eight yards.

The next day six.

And other things filled the days: the need for steady driving of the ship, and whispered consultations up and down the benches.

They needed a heat source, something that would blaze at 500 degrees, jangling, dazzling and confusing the senses of their captors. But it was an armed merchantman, a warship, and warships have nothing on board that will burn. Their poor clothing heaped together and somehow ignited would make a smoldering little fire, doing more damage to the human beings by its smoke than to the A'rkhov-Yar by its heat.

Barker went exploring in the cargo spaces. Again and again he was passed in the corridors by crew "men." Huddling against the glowing bulbs, choking down his rage and fear, he imitated the paint on the walls, and sometimes they broke their stride for a puzzled moment, sometimes not.

In a cargo space on the next day he found cases labeled with worms of plastic as "attention sticks" or possibly "arresting or halting tubes."

They were the close equivalent of railroad flares in appearance. He worked the tight-fitting cap of one to the point where he felt gritty friction. A striking surface——but he did not dare strike and test it. These things would have to put out hundreds of degrees of heat, or, if they were intended for use at any appreciable distance, thousands. They were thermal shrieks; they would be heard from one end of the ship to the other. In three trips he smuggled 140 of the sticks back to the propulsion room. Stoss helped him distribute them among the seats. He grimly told the lack-luster eyes and loose mouths: "If anybody pulls off one of the caps before I say so, I am going to hit the pain button and hold it down for five minutes."

They understood it for the death threat it was.

"Today's the day, I think," said Stoss in a whisper as Lakhrut made his benevolent entrance. "He sensed something yesterday at four meters. Today it's going to be three."

Barker pushed his little food cart, fingering the broken-off knob of a propulsion chair resting on its lower tray. He moved past Third Seat, Second Tier, Lakhrut behind him. The mad young man rose, picked up his plate and pretended to throw it at the cyclops.

Lakhrut drew his side-arm and blew the young man's head into a charred lump. "Oliver!" he cried, outraged. "Why did you not report that one of your units was becoming deranged? You should have put him through the space-lock days ago!"

"Oliver's" reply was to pace off a precise four meters and hurl the broken-off knob at the monster. He took a full windup, and rage for five thousand years of slavery and theft drove his muscles. The cyclops eye broke and spilled; the cyclops staggered in circles, screaming. Barker closed in, twisted the side-arm from the monster's convulsed hand and gave him what Third Seat, Second Tier, had got.

The roomful of men and women rose in terror, screaming.

"Quiet!" he yelled at them. "I've talked to some of you about this. You saw what happened. Those things are blind! You can strike them from five yards away and they'll never know what hit them."

He snatched up one of the fusees and rasped off the cap; it began to flare pulsatingly, not very bright, but intensely hot. He held it at arm's length and it scorched the hair on the back of his hand. "These things will dazzle what sensory equipment they do have," he yelled, "and you can confuse them with noise. They'll be coming to get us in a minute. All you have to do is make noise and mill around. You'll see what happens when they come for us—and then we'll go hunting!"

IN LESS than a minute his prediction was verified. A squad of the cyclops crew burst in, and the screaming of the Earth people left nothing to be desired; the creatures recoiled as if they had struck a wall. From six meters away Barker and the Stosses carefully ignited the flares and tossed them into the squad. They made half-hearted efforts to fire into the source of the trouble, but they were like men in a darkened boiler works—whose darkness was intermittently relieved by intolerable magnesium flares. Lakhrut's side-arm made short work of the squad.

Barker ripped their weapons from their fingers and demanded: "Who wants one? Who wants to go hunting? Not you, Miss Trimble; we'll need you for later. Stay in at safe place. Who's ready for a hunting party?"

One by one, twitching creatures remembered they were men and came up to take their weapons.

The first hunting party worked its way down a corridor hurling fusees, yelling and firing. The bag was a dozen cyclops, a dozen more weapons.

They met resistance at a massive door with a loophole. Blasts from a hand weapon leaped through the loophole, blind but deadly. Three of them fell charging the door.

"Warm it up for them," Stoss said. He snatched a dozen fusees, ducked under the fire and plastered himself against the door. Meticulously he uncapped the sticks and leaned them against the door, one by one.

The blast of heat drove Barker and his party back down the corridor, Stoss did not collapse until he had ignited the last flare, and wrenched open the door with a seared hand.

Through the door could be seen staggering cyclops figures, clawing blindly at the compartment walls. The Earthmen leaped through the brief, searing heat of the dozen flares and burned them down.

In the A'rkhov-Yar language, a terrified voice spoke over the ship public address system: "To the leader of the rebels! To the leader of the rebels! Return to your propulsion room and your crimes will be forgiven! Food will be doubled and the use of the Pain discontinued!"

Barker did not bother to translate. "Let's head for the navigation room," he said. "Try to save a couple of them."

One hour later he was telling the commander and Gori: "You two will set courses for Earth. You will work separately, and if your results don't agree we will put you each in a chair and hold down the button until you produce results that do agree. We also have a lady able to check on your mathematics, so don't try anything."

"You are insane," said the commander. "Other ships will pursue and destroy you."

"Other ships," Barker corrected him, "will pursue and fail to overtake us. I doubt very much that slave ships can overtake a ship driven by free men and women going home."

"We will attack openly for this insolence," snorted Gori. "Do you think you can stand against a battle fleet?

We will destroy your cities until you've had enough, and then use you as the slaves you are."

"I'm sure you'll try," said Barker. "However, all I ask is a couple of weeks for a few first-rate Ph.D.'s to go over this ship and its armaments. I believe you'll find you have a first-rate war on your hands, gentlemen. We don't steal; we *learn*.

"And now, if you please, start figuring that course. *You're* working for *us* now."

THE END

If you've enjoyed this book, you will not want to miss these terrific titles...

ARMCHAIR SCI-FI, & HORROR DOUBLE NOVELS, $12.95 each

D-1 **THE GALAXY RAIDERS** by William P. McGivern
SPACE STATION #1 by Frank Belknap Long

D-2 **THE PROGRAMMED PEOPLE** by Jack Sharkey
SLAVES OF THE CRYSTAL BRAIN by William Carter Sawtelle

D-3 **YOU'RE ALL ALONE** by Fritz Leiber
THE LIQUID MAN by Bernard C. Gilford

D-4 **CITADEL OF THE STAR LORDS** by Edmund Hamilton
VOYAGE TO ETERNITY by Milton Lesser

D-5 **IRON MEN OF VENUS** by Don Wilcox
THE MAN WITH ABSOLUTE MOTION by Noel Loomis

D-6 **WHO SOWS THE WIND...** by Rog Phillips
THE PUZZLE PLANET by Robert A. W. Lowndes

D-7 **PLANET OF DREAD** by Murray Leinster
TWICE UPON A TIME by Charles L. Fontenay

D-8 **THE TERROR OUT OF SPACE** by Dwight V. Swain
QUEST OF THE GOLDEN APE by Ivar Jorgensen and Adam Chase

D-9 **SECRET OF MARRACOTT DEEP** by Henry Slesar
PAWN OF THE BLACK FLEET by Mark Clifton.

D-10 **BEYOND THE RINGS OF SATURN** by Robert Moore Williams
A MAN OBSESSED by Alan E. Nourse

ARMCHAIR SCIENCE FICTION CLASSICS, $12.95 each

C-1 **THE GREEN MAN**
by Harold M. Sherman

C-2 **A TRACE OF MEMORY**
By Keith Laumer

C-3 **INTO PLUTONIAN DEPTHS**
by Stanton A. Coblentz

ARMCHAIR MASTERS OF SCIENCE FICTION SERIES, $16.95 each

M-1 **MASTERS OF SCIENCE FICTION, Vol. One**
Bryce Walton—"Dark of the Moon" and other tales

M-2 **MASTERS OF SCIENCE FICTION, Vol. Two**
Jerome Bixby: "One Way Street" and other tales

If you've enjoyed this book, you will not want to miss these terrific titles…

ARMCHAIR SCI-FI & HORROR DOUBLE NOVELS, $12.95 each

D-21   **EMPIRE OF EVIL** by Robert Arnette
        THE SIGN OF THE TIGER by Alan E. Nourse & J. A. Meyer

D-22   **OPERATION SQUARE PEG** by Frank Belknap Long
        ENCHANTRESS OF VENUS by Leigh Brackett

D-23   **THE LIFE WATCH** by Lester Del Rey
        CREATURES OF THE ABYSS by Murray Leinster

D-24   **LEGION OF LAZARUS** by Edmond Hamilton
        STAR HUNTER by Andre Norton

D-25   **EMPIRE OF WOMEN** by John Fletcher
        ONE OF OUR CITIES IS MISSING by Irving Cox

D-26   **THE WRONG SIDE OF PARADISE** by Raymond F. Jones
        THE INVOLUNTARY IMMORTALS by Rog Phillips

D-27   **EARTH QUARTER** by Damon Knight
        ENVOY TO NEW WORLDS by Keith Laumer

D-28   **SLAVES TO THE METAL HORDE** by Milton Lesser
        HUNTERS OUT OF TIME by Joseph E. Kelleam

D-29   **RX JUPITER SAVE US** by Ward Moore
        BEWARE THE USURPERS by Geoff St. Reynard

D-30   **SECRET OF THE SERPENT** by Don Wilcox
        CRUSADE ACROSS THE VOID by Dwight V. Swain

ARMCHAIR SCIENCE FICTION CLASSICS, $12.95 each

C-7   **THE SHAVER MYSTERY, Book One**
      by Richard S. Shaver

C-8   **THE SHAVER MYSTERY, Book Two**
      by Richard S. Shaver

C-9   **MURDER IN SPACE** by David V. Reed
      by David V. Reed

ARMCHAIR MASTERS OF SCIENCE FICTION SERIES, $16.95 each

M-3   **MASTERS OF SCIENCE FICTION, Vol. Three**
      Robert Sheckley, "The Perfect Woman" and other tales

M-4   **MASTERS OF SCIENCE FICTION, Vol. Four**
      Mack Reynolds, "Stowaway" and other tales

If you've enjoyed this book, you will not want to miss these terrific titles…

ARMCHAIR SCI-FI & HORROR DOUBLE NOVELS, $12.95 each

D-41   **FULL CYCLE** by Clifford D. Simak
        IT WAS THE DAY OF THE ROBOT by Frank Belknap Long

D-42   **THIS CROWDED EARTH** by Robert Bloch
        REIGN OF THE TELEPUPPETS by Daniel Galouye

D-43   **THE CRISPIN AFFAIR** by Jack Sharkey
        THE RED HELL OF JUPITER by Paul Ernst

D-44   **PLANET OF DREAD** by Dwight V. Swain
        WE THE MACHINE by Gerald Vance

D-45   **THE STAR HUNTER** by Edmond Hamilton
        THE ALIEN by Raymond F. Jones

D-46   **WORLD OF IF** by Rog Phillips
        SLAVE RAIDERS FROM MERCURY by Don Wilcox

D-47   **THE ULTIMATE PERIL** by Robert Abernathy
        PLANET OF SHAME by Bruce Elliot

D-48   **THE FLYING EYES** by J. Hunter Holly
        SOME FABULOUS YONDER by Phillip Jose Farmer

D-49   **THE COSMIC BUNGLARS** by Geoff St. Reynard
        THE BUTTONED SKY by Geoff St. Reynard

D-50   **TYRANTS OF TIME** by Milton Lesser
        PARIAH PLANET by Murray Leinster

ARMCHAIR SCIENCE FICTION CLASSICS, $12.95 each

C-13   **SUNKEN WORLD**
        by Stanton A. Coblentz

C-14   **THE LAST VIAL**
        by Sam McClatchie, M. D.

C-15   **WE WHO SURVIVED (THE FIFTH ICE AGE)**
        by Sterling Noel

ARMCHAIR MASTERS OF SCIENCE FICTION SERIES, $16.95 each

MS-5   **MASTERS OF SCIENCE FICTION, Vol. Five**
        Winston K. Marks—Test Colony and other tales

MS-6   **MASTERS OF SCIENCE FICTION, Vol. Six**
        Fritz Leiber—Deadly Moon and other tales

If you've enjoyed this book, you will not want to miss these terrific titles...

ARMCHAIR SCI-FI & HORROR DOUBLE NOVELS, $12.95 each

www.ingramcontent.com/pod-product-compliance
Lightning Source LLC
Chambersburg PA
CBHW050323200626
46810CB00022B/1035